THE HAUNTING HAND

The Haunting Hand

W. Adolphe Roberts

MYSTERIOUSPRESS.COM

INTEGRATED MEDIA
NEW YORK

Originally published in 1926.

Cover design by Amanda Shaffer.

ISBN: 978-1-5040-9395-8

This edition published in 2024 by MysteriousPress.com/Open Road Integrated Media, Inc.
180 Maiden Lane
New York, NY 10038
www.openroadmedia.com

INTRODUCTION

The Haunting Hand is the first novel by W(alter) Adolphe Roberts (1886–1962) and is generally credited with being the first mystery novel by a Black writer. It is one of five mystery novels produced in a prolific career spent mainly as a journalist, travel writer, and activist on behalf of Jamaica.

Born a primarily white octoroon in Kingston, Jamaica, his father was a successful businessman, largely as a silk merchant, planter, and clergyman, providing sufficient wealth to have his son privately educated. The young Roberts moved to the United States in 1904. He tried his hand at poetry but made his career as a journalist, including working at the prestigious *Daily Gleaner* when he was only sixteen. He then was hired by a New York newspaper to serve as a war correspondent in France during World War I and began an affair with the famous sociologist Margaret Sanger in 1916.

He returned to New York to take over the editorship of *Ainslee's*, a magazine of fiction and poetry, where he championed Edna St. Vincent Millay, before joining the staff of the hugely successful *Hearst's International Magazine.*

He became a successful essayist, historian, and lecturer who also wrote nearly a dozen novels. Curiously, few of his books, whether fiction or non-fiction, are set in Jamaica. The fact is curious because Roberts became perhaps the era's most vocal supporter for Jamaican independence from the British government, founding the Jamaican Progressive League in New York in 1936, lecturing, and writing countless pamphlets in support of self-governance.

For his efforts, the Queen of England awarded him the prestigious order of Member of the British Empire in 1961. He had made enemies in the movement, however, who doubted that Jamaica was ready and organized enough for independence when it was declared the following year and the new Jamaican Constitution banned him from any involvement in Jamaica's parliamentary affairs.

He had maintained dual citizenship and returned to live in Jamaica when he was sixty-five and died in 1962, the year his dream and efforts succeeded.

His political crusade largely ended his career as a novelist, as he wrote only four more mysteries after *The Haunting Hand* (1926)—*The Mind Reader* (1929) and *The Top-Floor Killer* (1935), under his own name, and two as Stephen Endicott, *Mayor Harding of New York* (1931) and *The Strange Case of Bishop Sterling* (1932).

The beginning of *The Haunting Hand* convincingly prepares the reader for a supernatural novel when a seemingly impossible event occurs. Margot Anstruther, a beautiful aspiring film actress, has thrown a party in her one-room New York City apartment for the cast of her movie and the director, Frederick Stoner, who has less-than-honorable intentions for her. She has also invited her boyfriend, Gene Valery, who adores her.

After everyone has gone, she collapses into her bed and lights a cigarette, dropping the match onto the floor. When she reaches down to be certain it has been extinguished, a hand reaches out from under her bed to grind it out. Petrified at who could be under her bed, convinced it must by a psychopath intending to kill her, she finally manages the courage to look and sees that no one is there. She reaches for the telephone and calls Gene, asking him to hurry over, speaking in French to fool the lurking murderer. When he arrives, he searches under the bed, and the entire apartment, to be certain no one is hidden in a corner, a closet, or anywhere else.

They call the police, who also do a thorough search but are convinced she was having a nightmare and are dismissive until one of them swears he has just seen the same thing.

When the tough and skeptical homicide detective shows up, she tells him of the young woman who had previously occupied the room who had walked away one day and was never seen again, and of another tenant in the rooming house who did the same thing almost immediately after the woman vanished.

Margot is soon able to conquer her fear and determines to solve the mystery, just as Sherlock Holmes would.

Roberts is able to sustain suspense in the early stages of the novel, and then presents Margot as a bright detective figure, both in terms of her observations and especially her deductions. A romance story is woven throughout.

It must be admitted that there are moments when the prose leaves a bit to be desired. While describing Gene, Roberts writes, "At time his smile quickened his face to actual beauty."

In another scene, he notes, ". . . Margot stood motionless, with an intangible, vague wonder in her groping mind."

Like many impossible crime stories and locked room mysteries, not to mention the hocus-pocus of skilled magicians, the author has established the notion that there could be no rational explanation for a seemingly other-worldly occurrence, only to explain how it could have been done—and that the girl really had not been sawed in half.

—Otto Penzler

THE HAUNTING HAND

CHAPTER I

MOVIE MEN AND MANNEQUINS

Mid October, with its tang, and the blazoned glory of its skies and sun and tawny trees! Margot Anstruther thanked a kind fate that she could live these brilliant, exhilarating days out of doors. Had she been confined to office or classroom, her restless spirit would have carried her body with it, in reckless escape. Long Island—where the Superfilm Company studio spread over the landscape—although not precisely the Maine woods or sea, or the open spaces of her own wide-flung West, at least spelled trees and grass and fresh air.

Margot stood on the diminutive roof-garden of her New York home, watching the moon rise over the house-tops. It was eight o'clock and her guests would soon arrive. She hoped that Gene Valery would come before the others. It was pleasant to be loved so ardently by Gene, but she surmised that it would be pleasanter if she could love as ardently in return. At any rate, his friendship was invaluable. He was the only one with whom she could share her mental gymnastics, the aspect of her mind which others would regard as rather too serious for human nature's daily food.

She had Gene to thank for her tiny roof-garden. It was one of those quaint affairs, a covering built over the yard, to be found in many an old New York house. Gene had rigged up a trellis and had brought potted palms and a South American hammock. For to-night he had hung Japanese lanterns. Margot had already lighted them. That small, mock garden took the curse, so to speak, off her lodging-house quarters, which consisted of one large, high-ceilinged room, in which she slept, ate—her breakfasts—and had her being.

She cut short her transport over the moon, stepped across the door-sill into the room, and cast critical eyes over her domain. A brass bed in one far corner was concealed by a screen, which Gene had made and she had decorated. The effect was rather good. She had recently acquired a divan, with many cushions, large and soft and gaily colored. Against one wall was a chest of drawers, a Chinese scarf over its battered top, a brass jar at one end, and a pewter candlestick with orange candle, at the other. The walls were a muddy gray, but there was a Japanese print here and there, and bright cretonne at the windows and on the wicker chairs.

Flanking the old-fashioned fireplace were her bookcases, built and painted by Gene. As catholic in her literary tastes as in her choice of friends, Margot's books presented a varied diet; fiction ranging from Kipling to Anatole France, poetry from Dante to Millay. A desk-table and an old console table—her own acquisitions—with carved wood book-racks for a few modern novels, and a bit of brass or copper; and two much worn but softly blended Oriental rugs thrown over the antiquated carpet, almost hiding its ugliness. Margot had achieved distinction, beauty and a subtle charm, in a room which previous tenants of the old lodging-house must have accepted as irretrievably barren and sordid.

She glanced in her four-foot mirror and patted her hair. It looked redder than usual in the light from the candles and from the yellow-shaded electric lamp over by the table. She flicked a speck of dust from the mirror-frame, gave a little twist to her soft, straight hung dress of corn color silk, then glanced toward the lanterns swinging in the evening breeze. Yes—it was all rather nice, but she was especially grateful for the roof-garden. Of course, a chilly October night could not be expected to lend exotic warmth to the scene, but in the room, the logs would be burning.

Six weeks since she had first met her expected guests: Frederick Stoner, the director of the Superfilm Company, with his strange, pale eyes; May Cheshire, the little blond girl who had been the first to inspire Margot with a desire to get into pictures; Lulu Leinster, the prize-beauty-contest winner from Texas, whose large brown eyes, beautifully chiseled lips and exquisite skin and yellow hair would have been assets in any profession. These three, and others, men and girls of the company, whose admiring friendship Margot had won during the past six weeks of work in the great studio of the Superfilm Company. Gene Valery was an older friend. That he happened to be an efficient young camera man with the same company was a pleasing coincidence.

Six weeks! A mere point in time, but they had been constructive weeks. To her own satisfaction and to that of her director, it had been proved that she had histrionic talent of a high order and that she screened admirably. Of no less significance the fact that she knew now, beyond all doubt, not only what she could do, but what she wanted to do. The absurd thing was that she should originally have chosen science as her profession!

Mentally equipped she might be for scientific work, but oh, how much more interesting it was to act! Certainly more remunerative. That morning in June, when she had applied for work and been taken on as an "extra" by the International, had supplied not only a little extra cash for her summer vacation but the fillip to her vague ambition to be a screen actress. And here she was, at twenty-five, launched on her career.

Her laboratory work would not be wasted; nothing excellent was ever wasted, she knew, and she was grateful for any acquisitive experience which she owed to her college course. But mental activities on the side, she would regard as a hobby; for an actress she was by temperament, and a good actress she proposed to be by intelligent use of her powers.

Funny, how Stoner had engaged her that day, and given her a real part in the new picture, *A Toreador's Love!* Funny how he had chosen her, instead of the lovely Lulu, for apparently no good reason! When Lulu proceeded to weep and look like a piece of broken Dresden china, he had weakened to the extent of giving the latter a very small role, but it was still a mystery to Margot why he had given *her* the important part for which she and Lulu—and many others—had applied, in response to an advertisement. She had forgotten, or hadn't had time, to tell Gene about it. She must remember to tell him sometime. It would amuse him and perhaps he'd be able to dispel the vague sense of mystery aroused in her by Stoner, with his strange pale eyes, from that first moment when she had given him her name and address.

Margot smiled, recalling Gene's absurd jealousy of Frederick Stoner. Ridiculous to suppose that she could ever give the director a second thought except in relation to her work. He wasn't a bad sort, really, but his rather brutish good looks repelled her. And he was a good director, although, as everyone had told her, he belonged to the old school of directors; very old-fashioned in his methods. There were few, if any, of his kind left in the motion picture industry, for which those working under him were devoutly thankful. Stoner's notion of discipline was to shout his orders and conduct himself generally as if everything were melodrama.

Gene was rather annoying with his jealous suspicions. She didn't dare tell him that she endured Stoner's boring attentions as much for Gene's sake as for her own. Stoner had never liked Gene, and now he made his dislike very evident. If she were to let it become obvious that she preferred Gene's friendship to Stoner's, the director would be quite capable of discharging him and queering him with other directors and managers. Men often did contemptible things out of jealousy. If she explained all this to Gene, ten to one he would resign, just when his chances for promotion were so good. Gene was a rank outsider. He had been taken on almost by accident and retained because he was so amazingly clever with the camera. But all the cleverness in the world wouldn't help you if you were an outsider and an influential director considered you undesirable.

Speaking of jealousy! She smiled again, remembering that the only member of the cast of *A Toreador's Love*, who had declined her invitation for to-night, was the star, Corinne Delamar. To be sure, she was younger than Corinne—somewhat—and perhaps prettier, but there was no reason for fearing that she had designs upon the director. Margot had treated Corinne with consistent and amiable courtesy, but had made no attempt to overcome her antagonism, by catering to her up-stage exactions. In token of her goodwill and to celebrate her success in the Superfilm's new picture, she had asked them all to her informal home for a "party." The word covered a multitude of sins—of excess or boredom. Silly of Corinne not to come! Silly of her to advertise her jealousy of Margot! There had been gossip about it already, some of it a trifle malicious.

At that point in her rapid reflections, Gene appeared, carrying a bunch of yellow roses. He brought candy also, and cigarettes, and a bottle or two under his arm. Gene was tall, clear-skinned and plain of feature, except for his blue eyes. He was well knit, had brilliant teeth and a smile which made one forget that his mouth was too wide and his nose crooked—it had been broken in a football game. At times his smile quickened his face to actual beauty.

With bright eyes smiling in unison with her red, parted lips, Margot watched him unwrap his packages. Then he stood looking at her, longing to take her in his arms, and daring only to stare at her adoringly.

"You *are* a darling, Gene!" Her voice cooed at him, and she took a step nearer, smiling at him.

Well, that wasn't so bad in the way of a greeting, his expansive smile told her.

"And *you* are a darling—an exquisite darling!"

She went a little nearer to him.

"If you won't muss me, and won't get too rapturous, I'll let you kiss me—*once*—just to give you a good start for the evening."

"Sweetheart!" Impetuously he tried to put an arm around her, then, gingerly, as she drew away with a laugh of warning, he put his hands on her shoulders and bending down, kissed her lips. It was a kiss pregnant with emotion but short-lived, as she freed herself, with another gay laugh.

"Look, Gene! You haven't even noticed my new divan and my lovely cushions."

He glanced at the divan without interest, turned his gaze back to Margot, and seeing her mouth droop in disappointment, he made an effort to smile approval.

"Bully, darling! It adds fifty per cent to this room." His eyes roved about. "Color scheme's fine!" His wandering glance reached the corner where the screen did not entirely conceal the large brass bed. "Why on earth don't you get rid of that incubus?"

Margot's smile clouded. "Now, you don't imagine I keep it for sheer love of the beastly thing? I told Mrs. Bellew that I was going to buy a divan, and she promised to remove that monster over there. But when the divan arrived the other day, she told me I'd have to keep the bed till she could have one of her rooms done over. I can't throw the darn thing out the window. It makes me *so* mad!"

"Sorry I mentioned it, dearest. Don't bother about it. That screen hides it and the room's so huge you can forget that corner."

"Anyway," she smiled cheerfully, "I've managed to cover her hideous old Wilton, except in spots, especially that torn place near the bed. Dad sent the Orientals from home. Worn a bit, but the coloring's lovely. She wouldn't take up her old carpet. Says the paint's off the floor and the boards cracked and rough. I don't believe she's had that carpet up for years."

"By the way," said Gene irrelevantly, "Stoner coming to-night?"

"Why, of course he is!"

"Precisely—*why*—'of course'?"

"How silly of you, Gene! I can't snub Stoner, and it would have been worse than a snub not to ask him to-night. Why, *he gave* me the job I'm celebrating! How *could* I leave him out?"

"Suppose you're right." Gene's agreement was sulky. "But I don't like Stoner and I hate to see him hanging around you."

She went up to him and gave him a light, swift kiss on the end of his chin, then ran back before he could seize her.

"Be a good sport, Gene, dear. A man of Stoner's type couldn't possibly hurt me in anyway, for I'd never want him as a friend, let alone as a lover. But it's policy to be decent to him, and I'm not a fool."

"All the same I hate to see his familiar manner with you. All the logic in the universe isn't going to change that."

"And I can't help *that!* If you *will* be jealous of an inferior, then you just prove an inferiority complex." Her smile sweetened the words, then she added with a laugh: "The same kind of complex that made Corinne Delamar decline my invitation for to-night."

Before Gene could reply, the door-bell rang. To Margot's relief, the first arrivals were May Cheshire and Lulu Leinster, with several other girls and men from *A Toreador's Love.* She was glad that Stoner had not come in time to make an embarrassing trio with Gene and herself.

Amid the chatter and laughter and admiring exclamations regarding Margot's room and the tiny roof-garden, the bell rang again. This time it would be Stoner, she knew. She ran to the door to admit him, standing with her back to the room.

Stoner was tall and heavily built, with thick eyebrows that gave him a fierce expression when he frowned. He was handsome, of a crude, slightly brutal type. He possessed, at least, that illusive quality, personality. He smiled down at Margot and extended a large, well-groomed hand.

Her cordial but impersonal greeting of: "Why, hello, Mr. Stoner! Awfully glad to see you!" sounded innocent enough, which was for Gene's benefit, but only Stoner saw the roguish, upturned corners of her mouth, and the smile of challenge in her lovely eyes. After all, one must play a game with finesse. If she didn't coquette a *little* with Stoner, just to keep the ball rolling, either she'd antagonize him, or run the risk of bringing on a crisis by goading him to a less oblique attack.

Before she turned and sauntered with him across the room, the color had deepened in her cheeks. Whenever Stoner looked at her with his critical, predatory eyes, Margot always grew uncomfortably conscious of her physical assets: of the long, gently curved lines of her body; of the clearness of her white skin, with its pink shadings; of the golden auburn of her bobbed hair; of her nose, straight, except for a slight uptilt at the end, which harmonized with the way her lips deepened and lifted at the corners of her mobile mouth. She had no unwarranted conceit, but the trained appraisal of Stoner's glance had brought to her to-night, as on previous occasions, the conviction that she was more beautiful than she had supposed.

An hour later, Margot, sitting Turk-fashion on her divan, and flashing a smile over the rim of her cocktail glass at the girls and men standing or lolling about the room, answered their toast to her success, with one of her own.

"If Shakespeare were alive to-day, he'd be writing scenarios, and instead of saying: 'The play's the thing!' he'd say: 'The movies are the *only* thing!' Drink to the drama of the screen! May it live long and prosper, and have lots of—of offspring!"

"Taking liberties with the famous old toast of Rip Van Winkle. Very clever of you, Margot, I'll tell the world!" It was Stoner speaking.

Surprising, Margot thought, that Stoner, with all his crudities, should have recognized her paraphrasing of the toast of Rip Van Winkle. She was sure that no one else but Gene in that room had education enough for that. She studied Stoner through lowered eyes. He was standing by the table, compounding bright-colored cocktails with much orange juice and not much gin. The bottles were emptying rather early in the evening.

Stoner, liking to be in evidence wherever there were pretty women about, had insisted upon presiding over the mixing of drinks. He swung the big shaker with a loud tinkling of ice, and boisterous jests thrown carelessly to one or another. He smiled, it seemed to Gene's watchful and jealous eyes, a little possessively at Margot, as he said, with a laugh:

"I'll hand it to you, Margot, for knowing how to maneuver the drinks so that we'll stay sober and yet enjoy ourselves. Most women, when they entertain, can't strike that happy medium. They're either stingy with the booze, or they turn on the hose and send you home wall-eyed. You're the perfect little entertainer, I'll tell the world."

"And why on earth, Margot, did you think you had to apologize for this room of yours?" Lulu glanced about with wondering admiration. "I call it a swell room, and fine for a party!"

Margot smiled, and her gray eyes twinkled.

"It's really just a bedroom, Lulu, as I warned you. I can't pretend it's anything else, while that monstrous brass bed stands over in that corner."

"Well, you've got it screened, haven't you?" Lulu argued.

"That's a weak camouflage. And when I go to bed, of course I remove the screen, and then, when I look around the room, I feel as if I were in a regular movie bedroom. They're always so funny, you know. Aren't they, Mr. Stoner?"

For a second his expression showed that he thought she might be making fun of him.

"We have to rig up those fancy bedrooms, to please the fans who've never seen a really swell bedroom in their lives. They think they're getting the real dope when we show them beds all covered with lace and satin and the Lord knows what not."

"Beds don't scare *me*," laughed May Cheshire, shaking her little blond, bobbed head. "Ain't they among our best little props? Ain't we jumpin' in and out of 'em in half the scenes?"

Margot laughed with the others. Hers was too human a sense

of humor to resent the obviousness of such an exhibition of another girl's wit. It was spontaneous at least.

"As to beds," Stoner evidently thought the subject not yet exhausted; "you aren't the only young actress, Margot, who's living in one room. Lots of them in the 'Roaring Forties.' I've seen rooms that weren't a patch on this one for looks and comfort, and I've sat on more beds than I could count, when there weren't enough chairs to go round."

"At least you won't be put to that trouble in my room."

Gene exulted at the slight coolness in her tone. Damn cheeky Stoner, with his remarks about sitting on beds. Stoner gave her a sharp look, then stared across the room to where the brass bed peeked around a corner of the screen.

"Wouldn't be any trouble, I assure you." What was it, in his voice? Irony, ridicule, effrontery or just plain nerve?

For the first time in weeks, Margot had a vivid memory of the look in Stoner's eyes when she had first given him her address, and the following day, when he first suggested calling on her. The impression of something vaguely sinister, had faded with more familiar knowledge of the man, and his amiable crudities of mind and manner.

"Guess you'll soon be movin' up town into some big swell flat on Riverside Drive. You'll be a star I bet, in the next picture they shoot." There was faint envy in Lulu's big blue eyes.

"If I move up town," said Margot, with a laugh, "it certainly won't be to Riverside Drive. Too many murders of young actresses and dancers in that neighborhood. And I'm in no hurry to move away from here. This house has atmosphere, hasn't it, Gene?" She turned her head to smile directly into Gene's watchful eyes. "It was built in the sixties, you know, Mr. Stoner." Her glance shifted to the director, who was sitting on the arm of an old chair, and imperiling its usefulness. "Picturesque old moldings, high ceilings and all that sort of thing. Don't you like these brownstone relics, Mr. Stoner?"

"Gene, there, knows more about them than I do. He has to shoot them every now and then. But the inside dope on architecture and periods is the bluff of the art director. 'Ain't it the truth,' Valery?"

Gene disdained to attempt the sort of repartee which Stoner could have understood. He got up, and poured himself a drink, and drank it unsociably, except for a glance over his glass at Margot. She decided hastily to make conversation of a kind that would entertain the crowd, and avoid personalities, and danger of sword crossing between Gene and Stoner. She would strike the note of mystery. That would intrigue them all, at a minimum of effort.

"Listen, people," she began, her mouth widening in a smile which included everyone. "The best thing about this house is that it makes good on its appearance. Mysterious lodgers have lived here. Strange things have happened here."

In her roving glance from one guest to the other, her eyes met Stoner's. Their pale blue looked dark in the shaded lighting of the room. He sat quite still, staring intently at her. Certainly the man had strange eyes. One moment colorless and without expression, even when his mouth suggested significant things when he smiled or spoke to her; the next moment taking on depth and color and a vague suggestion of mystery. She was conscious of a slight effort in withdrawing her glance from his arresting gaze.

Lulu dragged her chair closer, and May sprang to the divan, and cuddled close to Margot.

"Do go on!" May's voice shrilled excitedly. "*What* strange things have happened here?"

"I only heard about it yesterday." Margot determined to keep her glance carefully away from Stoner's direction. He made her nervous for some reason. "I was talking to the landlady—trying to get her to take away her old brass bed. She told me that a girl who was living in this very room, disappeared in the funniest way, about three months ago. She didn't just walk out, bag and baggage. She disappeared—literally. Left all her belongings, even her comb and tooth brush. *And*—she's never come back!"

"That's interesting!" Stoner's comment came as he walked to the table and poured a drink. His back was turned to Margot. "What Sort of a girl was she?" He stood now facing the others, and looking at Margot. He frowned as if mentally groping with an abstract problem. "Anybody have a drink?" he added genially.

Cries from the girls, begging for silence, and telling the men to pour drinks, if they must, without talking about it or inter-rupting Margot's story; then silence and absorbed attention as Margot continued:

"The girl's name was Stella Ball. She was supposed to be working at Macy's, half time, in the afternoons. But Mrs. Bellew communicated with the manager at Macy's, after the girl left here, and they'd never even heard of her!"

Stoner leisurely blew rings of smoke from his cigarette, and said lazily:

"She may have been run over in the street. Obscure people often disappear that way. Sudden accident, and no identifica-tion possible. No papers on them, and nobody claims them at the morgue. Nothing so mysterious about that."

"Wait till you hear the rest of it!" Margot's eager glance avoided the chair where Stoner was lounging. "The very same day that the girl left here, an elderly man named Murchison, who had a garret room on the top floor, also disappeared, with equal finality."

"A *really* old man?" Lulu's instinct for romance jumped to the obvious conclusion.

"No, dear, just middle-aged. He was about fifty-five. Agile and wiry, Mrs. Bellew says. Young in Strength, but very unprepossessing. He was round-shouldered, and had a thin, ugly, hatchet sort of face. No girl could have looked twice at him. And in the evenings he stuck in his rooms like a hermit, and he seemed to hate women."

"Did he have a job anywhere?" someone asked.

"Nobody knows. He never gave any information about himself. Of course landladies like Mrs. Bellew would draw blood out of a stone, in the way of gossip, but, apparently, she never found out anything about that particular lodger. She didn't care, so long as he gave no trouble and paid his rent regularly."

"Perhaps the old bird had money, and the girl, Stella, may have fallen for that." Lulu's sense of romance was not to be crushed.

"Nonsense, Lulu. He wasn't a miser, with bags of gold in his trunk. He went out every day, so presumably he worked somewhere, but, judging by the way he lived, he certainly earned very little."

"Call it a case of hypnotism, and be done with it!" Stoner's suggestion came flippantly.

Margot turned her head quickly, and again met Stoner's eyes, staring at her through the shadows of the room, and the smoke from his cigarette.

"I thought of that. But the man's only motive in hypnotizing the girl would have been an immoral one, which wouldn't have required his taking her out of the house. No one here bothers about his neighbors. You could literally get away with murder, and not a soul be the wiser."

"Gosh! Catch *me* living in a spooky place like this!" May glanced over her shoulder, at the darker corner of the room where the brass bed hid its plebeian head.

"Speaking of mysteries!" Margot glanced with surprise at Gene, whose voice had broken the momentary silence in the room.—"Any of you happen to read about the disappearance from the Fellowe Institute, of a fraction of a gram of radium, a few months ago?"

"Yes, I read about it," said Margot eagerly. "They haven't the faintest idea who took it, but of course it was stolen. Any of you know anything about radium?" She glanced from one to another.

"Not a damn thing. I'll speak for the crowd." It was Stoner's voice, bland, a little ironical. "We motion picture people, Margot, aren't wise to all that scientific stuff. Ain't it the truth?" He laughed, throwing his glance around the room.

"Aren't you even interested when you read of such things in the papers, Mr. Stoner?" Margot regarded him with curious eyes. He was such a strange contradiction, with his unexpected knowledge along some lines, and his equally surprising lack of it along others.

"Can't say I am. As a matter of fact, I don't have much time for reading, except of course movie fan stuff, and the sports columns, and local politics and all the bunk they write and call dramatic criticism."

"But a thing like the disappearance of that radium is most interesting news. Even a tiny bit of radium is worth a lot of money, and they've had detectives on the case without getting a glimmer of light or a single clue."

"The odd part of it is," went on Gene, "that no one but an employee could have access to their stock of radium, and the mystery lies in the difficulty entailed in concealing it and getting out of the building with it. It seems that all persons engaged in work at the Institute are subject to search before they leave the building."

Margot could see by their faces that, so far as the others were concerned, the subject of radium was exhausted. But her own mystery narrative still held interest, She felt sure.

"Well, to get back to the girl Stella, and old Murchison—" began Margot.

"Why get back to them?" Stoner drawled the words, and rolled his eyes in comic supplication. "Much better turn on the jazz and let me shake another round of Bronxes."

"Righto!" laughed Margot, getting up and going toward the victrola. Without looking at Stoner she added:

"Evidently, Mr. Stoner, you haven't got the detective sort of mind."

"Have you?"

Through the high-pitched chatter of the girls, and the deeper cadence of the men's voices, Margot heard the brief, low-toned question. She turned around, facing Stoner.

"Yes, I have. Ever since I've been old enough to read, I've had a slant for mystery and detective stories. I adore unraveling mysteries."

"Is that so?" Stoner's drawl expressed tolerant amusement. The slight scorn so often shown by rather ignorant men for intelligent, women.

Margot put on a record, wound the victrola, then walked slowly to where Stoner stood. She let him light a cigarette for her as she said, smilingly:

"Ever read 'The House and the Brain,' by Bulwer-Lytton? Fascinating and gruesome. In fact quite blood-curdling."

"Any more so than Monsieur Dupin?"

"Oh, mercy, yes." She saw Gene approaching, and included him in the conversation. "Who's *your* favorite, Gene, in detective fiction?"

"Gaboriau," said Gene briefly, "and Maurice le Blanc."

"They would be," laughed Margot. "You're of French descent, and I suppose you read them in the original. Well, as for me, I vote for Conan Doyle's immortal Sherlock! Although I'll admit that Le Blanc's 'Memoirs of Arsene Lupin' are thrilling and clever."

"You and Valery are some pair of high-brows to be in the motion picture industry." Stoner sounded sarcastic, and Gene frowned darkly, but Margot answered gaily:

"I've never heard detective fiction called highbrow before. Except, of course, that I take it more seriously than most readers do, Mr. Stoner. You see, I was a medical student and specialized in chemistry before you gave me the chance of my young life to become an actress. I've had lots of fun analyzing the methods of most of the great fiction detectives. How's that?" Her upturned face challenged him with a bright smile.

"Hot stuff for your press agent, when I'm directing you as a star, some day."

Gene turned abruptly on his heel. Margot stood, her eyes held by Stoner's veiled scrutiny. For veiled it was; that expressed it exactly. For a few seconds his gaze held hers, then—again—what was it—that sudden dilating of the pupil; the queer overtone as of a yellowish shadow darkening the pale blue of the iris; a shimmer in the eyeball, like dust specks seen in a sunbeam. . . .

Margot lowered her head, and walked slowly to the door leading to the roof garden. Strange eyes! A little shiver shook her bare shoulders. The night was sultry. The room was heavy with smoke and the warm essence from many human bodies.

CHAPTER II

THE GRISLY HAND AND THE FLAME

As Margot danced, with one man and then another, a rapt, detached, impersonal joy, shone in her face. Gone, between her and her guests, the feeling of inequality that her agile and probing mind, had inspired for a short interval. Gone the sense in her of repugnance for Stoner, even when she danced in his arms. Gone the memory of his strange and disturbing eyes. Caught up in the rhythm of jazz, what mattered anything but motion—to these children of the Twentieth Century—the poetry of motion, the only poetry most of them would ever give a brass farthing for.

What if the music were secondhand? Syncopation and the phonograph record had come into being at the same time, and had swept away with a single victorious gesture the sentiment of the waltz, and the cooperation of eager fingers flying over a white keyboard. Here were new measures, mechanical, but satisfying and inspiring to youngsters of the Jazz Age.

But it was after midnight, and high time to respect the rule that all noise cease at twelve o'clock. Even in free-and-easy old houses such as this one, there was a limit. Sandwiches and salad and coffee, appeared mysteriously from a closet, where Margot concealed an electric plate. One more round of drinks, mutual toasts and eager congratulations to Margot for the success of her party, then the girls began to fumble with their wraps.

At the door, Stoner held out his hand for a second clasp. He had already shaken her hand in good-night. He had managed to be the last to leave the room. Even Gene had followed the others down the stairs, although he had maneuvered a whispered entreaty into her ear, to permit him to return in a few minutes, and she had yielded to the unhappiness in his eyes.

Stoner, holding her hand, looked down at her with a slow smile parting his thick lips.

"Grand success, your little party—Margot." She smiled, without attempting to withdraw her hand.

"Awfully glad you enjoyed it. Next time I promise to have the cocktails strong enough to suit you, Mr. Stoner."

"They were strong enough. Too strong, maybe, for those other little girls. You'd already stirred them up thoroughly with your story of mystery and murder."

Her eyes widened. "My story didn't include a murder."

"Well, it was hinted at—left to the imagination."

"Entirely so."

"Well, see here, little girl. Take my advice and cut out all that detective stuff. It fills your mind with truck and it's bad for your work. Take it from me, it is!"

"I'll write a mystery story myself, and perhaps you'll let me star in it. How about that, Mr. Director?" She laughed and tried to withdraw her hand.

"Nothing doing. Don't like mystery pictures. Well, good-by

and don't get nervous sleeping all alone in that big bed over there."

For a second, Margot felt angry resentment at what, on the lips of such a man as Stoner, might so easily contain an ugly meaning—a raw suggestion. The next second, meeting his eyes, so mysteriously contradictory to the insidious sensuality of his mouth, she knew that he had meant nothing insulting by his reference to her sleeping alone in the large bed. Perhaps he had no meaning at all, back of his words or his eyes, but there it was again, unsuspected by him, that strange, disturbing filming of the pale blue iris, and the dilation of the pupil. What in Heaven's name did it mean!

As Margot stood perfectly still, with the handle of the closed door in her hand, listening to the sound of Stoner's feet descending the uncarpeted stairs, the vague wonder and unrest she had felt before, became a concrete sensation of something very much like fear, yet fear of what! Not Stoner himself. That would be too absurd! Besides, the only thing a woman would have to be on her guard against with Stoner, concerned matters wherein lay no mystery whatever. There was never any mystery for a woman, attending the manifest gloating desire of a man. Certainly she could handle Stoner. That wasn't it. Well, what was it? She felt half tempted to talk it over with Gene. But hearing his step outside the door, she decided suddenly that she would not, could not, discuss Stoner with Gene.

Gene threw hat and coat on a chair in the manner of one who is anxious to dispose of superfluous incumbrance, and be strong for his swim against the current. He stood with his back to the wall, near the door, ignoring Margot's gesture toward a chair. Reading determination in his grave, young face, Margot lighted a cigarette, just to have something to finger, and walked toward him, in comic imitation of Carmen, arms akimbo, swaying of the torso, head tilted back, and a tantalizing smile on her lips. It was too late for melodrama, or even mild dramatics. She must treat Gene with friendly levity, or she'd have a heavy discussion to deal with.

"Why so black in your looks, milord? You frighten me with your beetling brows and acid smile?"

"Smile! I'm far from smiling, Margot."

She shrugged her shoulders. Gene in this mood had no more sense of humor than a clam.

"Don't be so darn literal, my dear boy. Of course you're not smiling. What I want to know is, why aren't you?"

"Because I'm too miserable, that's why, if you want to know."

"Now see here, Gene. In plain language, what's eating you? Haven't I been sweet to you to-night? I danced with you more than with any other man, and I talked with you a lot."

"It's that man Stoner. I'm not exactly blind."

"What is there not to be blind to?"

"He's a loud-mouthed motion picture man of the old school. Out of your class a thousand miles. But he's your director, and he's got the gall to have fallen in love with you, and makes no bones about letting us all know it."

"Rot! Tommy Rot! I suppose he admires me—in a way—but I've a hunch that his interest in me isn't really as *personal* as it seems to be."

Gene frowned at her. "Now what do you mean by that cryptic remark?"

Margot did not answer at once, then she said slowly:

"I don't know myself exactly what I mean. But the main thing for you, Gene, to get into that otherwise intelligent head of yours is, that even if Stoner *is* in love with me, I'm not and never could be, in love with *him*."

Gene looked neither convinced nor comforted.

"Men like Stoner aren't easily discouraged. I've seen him go after women before. It's just possible you might succumb to his cave-man technique in the end."

"'Technique'!" Margot laughed. "That's funny. He hasn't got any, that's one reason why I've got no use for him. He's awfully crude. Never lets me forget that he gave me my job. And speaking of technique, old dear, you'd better improve your own. It's terribly flattering, of course, to have a man jealous of you, but it's almost insulting to think that I could care for Stoner."

Gene studied her morosely for a moment, then he turned away and walked the length of the room. Margot's eyes, watching him, softened and she said gently:

"I forgive you, Gene."

Quickly he turned on his heel and approached her, his hands outstretched. He seized hers and held them close.

"Jealousy is always stupid, dear, but when a man's as much in love as I am, things get out of focus. I'm obsessed by a very human male desire to take care of you, Margot. To protect you against the world in general and men like Stoner in particular."

Margot smiled into his eager face.

"But, my dear. I can look after myself at present, as well as you could look after me."

He frowned and dropped her hands.

"I wasn't speaking in terms of dollars and cents. I meant a different sort of protection, the kind marriage to a decent man, gives a girl. And as to the rest of it: With fair luck I'll be a director before long."

Margot put her hand on his arm and gave it a little squeeze.

"That was crude of me, Gene. Forgive me. I really meant that we're both too young and unsettled to marry. I want to make good first, quite on my own. If I don't make the grade—a star, you know—and if I grow old and ugly," the very thought of it made her laugh gaily, "why *then* I really might need you, Gene, but by that time, being a mere man, of course you wouldn't *want* me."

He drew her nearer to him and his eyes darkened with emotion.

"I'd always want you, darling, and you could never be old or ugly to me."

"Where oh where have I heard those words before! Something strangely familiar about them." She laughed, then sobered quickly as Gene drew back, hurt by her levity.

"I'm only teasing, dear, but you must admit, if you've got a sense of humor, that it *is* awfully funny how every man when he's in love, always tells the woman that she could never be old or ugly to *him*."

"You can't imagine that an occasional man might mean it when he says it?" Gene spoke a little coldly.

"Why, my dear, they *all* mean it! That's the funniest part of it."

Gene reached for his hat and coat.

"You seem determined to squelch any sentiment between us to-night."

"To-night—yes. It's fearfully late, Gene, dear, and you must go, really."

He turned toward the door without a word, nor any attempt to caress her. A cynical man of the world could not have chosen a surer way of putting the initiative into the woman's hands. Margot moved a little nearer to him, then she said:

"You may kiss me good-night, Gene."

Gene was too much in love to play the game dexterously. He dropped hat and coat and took her eagerly into his arms. For a short moment she relaxed in his embrace and even kissed him with instinctive response to his passion. Then, as she turned her head away from his encroaching kisses, a sudden thought stilled his passion. He looked at her with troubled eyes.

"Darling, I can't bear to think of you living alone here, after what you told us about this house. You're taking chances and it worries me horribly."

"Don't be absurd, Gene. And remember, I have my own telephone, right by my bed. I'm indebted for that to the women who occupied this room after Stella Ball left. It's expensive but convenient."

"I'm glad it's by your bed. Easy to get at, if you wanted to call the police."

"'Police'!" she echoed with a laugh. "You're determined to stage a melodrama. If it got to the point of having to call the police I guess I'd be beyond help."

"Seriously, Margot, I'm anxious. Let me give you a ring in the next half hour. I shan't sleep unless I hear your voice before you drop off yourself."

"Idiot!" She gave him a playful shove in the direction of the door. "Don't you dare call me this time of night—morning, really. I'll be in bed before you've turned the corner, and sound asleep before you've used your latchkey."

An hour later, Margot, with a weary sigh disposed of the last plate and spoon, and emptied the ashes out of the last overflowing ash tray. She undressed and tip-toed to the bathroom for a shower. It would be a cold one at that hour, and it would make her wakeful, but she felt stuffy and cigarette smoke seemed to have penetrated right through her clothes. A few strokes of the brush over her thick bobbed hair, then she gave another sigh, of comfort this time, as she propped up her pillows, took a book from the night table and lighted a cigarette. She was so wide awake she knew that she would have to read herself into a relaxed state of mind. She kept a dull novel on hand to act as a sleeping potion, for often she found it difficult to quiet her active mind.

The book wobbled in her hand, and her eyelids drooped. But she wasn't quite sleepy enough yet, so she clutched the book a little tighter. The cigarette trembled between her lips and almost fell. She put it on the ash tray, squeezing the lighted end. Then—droop, droop of the eyelids, and she let the book fall to the coverlet. But the electric light! Oh, dear! She must reach out and snap the thing off. Perhaps the very slight muscular exertion of moving her arm, and pulling the chain, stirred the nerves at the base of her brain. Darkness, and stillness, yet that delightful drowsiness was gone.

A faint ray of light came through the window opening on the roof-garden. It was from a distant street lamp. It left the shadows on either side of it the more dense. Perhaps another puff at her cigarette would be enough to soothe her wakefulness. She reached out and took it from the tray, picked up a match and lighted what was left of her cigarette.

A puff as she held the match to it then, more asleep than awake, Margot stretched her arm over the side of the bed, and dropped the still burning match to the floor. The next second and she was once more alert. A lighted paper match on a thin, worn old rug! She had seen the evil little things burn holes in tables, and the edges of mantels, and she had ruined the handle of a good knife with the careless dropping of a lighted match. Vaguely these things went through her mind as she leaned over the side of the bed and looked for the match.

Her outstretched hand was poised above the coverlet. She had located the match and had put out her arm to reach down for it. Then—without sound, almost it seemed to her petrified gaze, without movement—a small, thin hand, then a forearm, reached out from under her bed.

Stricken with terror, her heart first missing a beat, then seeming to be in her throat, strangling her, Margot watched the hand reach to the match and tap, it softly with thin fingers, crushing the burning end. Then—back, without sound, back whence it had come, disappearing under the bed.

Margot lay rigid, eyes staring into the darkness, lips parted and stiff. The first paralysis of horror at the incredible thing she had seen, quickened to a definite and agonized fear—a personal and feminine fear.

Someone—a man of course—was under the bed. He must have been there all the evening. He had tapped the lighted match because it might have set fire to the rug, and led to his discovery. He didn't think she had seen him reach out for the flame. He'd wait till he was sure she was asleep, then he'd come creeping out—creeping—creeping—

Burglary! Ridiculous! Margot's clever brain could function, in spite of her fear. Surely no New York burglar would hide in a house for hours where all the rooms were occupied! He would break in when all was still and safe. Besides, what had she, or anyone living in such a house, that a burglar would want? It was not theft. She felt sure of that. A maniac—an escaped maniac, a paranoiac, who had picked her out as the one on whom to avenge an imagined grievance. As a medical student she had come to know the possibilities where paranoiacs were concerned.

Murder! That's what it was. Murder! God in Heaven, how long would the creature wait? She dared not scream, and who would hear her if she did? Walls and doors in that old house were so thick as to be almost sound-proof. She'd go mad if she had to endure this suspense much longer! If she were to break down and become hysterical, that would be the end, right there! Whatever she did, she *must* keep a cool head!

A violent wrench of nerves and muscles and will, then she raised a hand that was icy cold and stiff, and switched on the light on the night table.

CHAPTER III

A CREATURE WITHOUT A BODY

The intense relief of sudden light in a dark room, when one has felt the grip of deadly fear; brought from Margot a long drawn breath that her quick wits changed to a yawn—an audible convincing yawn, convincing to whatever, whoever, waited with the stillness of death, under her bed.

Determined not to lose self-control, rapid and coherent thought brought a sequence of small acts calculated to ward off immediate danger and arrest suspicion in the maniacal creature whose hand and arm she had seen. By this time Margot was convinced that she had to deal with a maniac of some description.

She followed up her yawn with a restless twist of her body on the mattress, a bang to her pillows, and finally a low grunt of physical discomfort which ended in a self-addressed murmur of:

"Gosh! Wish I could get to sleep!"

Her next move was to seize her book and turn the pages

noisily. Would it be possible, she wondered, to keep on turning pages until dawn,—possible for her to retain her self-control as the suspense grew more and more unbearable, and would it be possible so far as the patience of her lurking enemy was concerned. Would It—she thought of the living thing as It—wait indefinitely for its proposed attack? Surely not. Then this was merely a respite. It might wait for hours for the light to be switched off again, but It would not wait for daybreak and the consequent danger of discovery.

She measured the distance to the door leading into the hall. It wasn't so far, and if she didn't get muscle-bound with fear, she could make it with one long spring. But even so, before she could open the door, there would be another spring—from the Other One under the bed, and It would catch her before she could turn the handle. And if not a spring, then a shot at her, for of course the creature must be armed. No! Even if she were to get out of bed in a leisurely, unsuspicious fashion, for whatever apparent purpose, she would be attacked as surely and swiftly as if she were to scream for help.

Horrible, this waiting and thinking and planning! Horrible this unseen menace—man or woman, sane or insane, violent or craven! There was a limit to what even her healthy nerves could endure without snapping.

A sudden memory of Gene begging to let him call her up. If only she had told him he might do so. Ridiculous! He would have rung her up an hour ago at least, and by now he was probably sound asleep. He had supposed that she was going immediately to bed, and would not have dared to risk disturbing her after this long interval, even if she had consented to let him call her.

A sudden alternative, a desperate expedient occurred to her with a quickening of her pulse. Why couldn't she call Gene! She would be taking a fearful chance, for the mere calling of Central might be the signal for an attack. To be sure, when calling for the police one had merely to say the one word to the operator, therefore an ordinary number would sound innocent enough. But how could she be sure that any such reasoning would occur to the mind of a maniac? The mere sound of her voice might be enough to bring that creeping, ghostly arm from under the bed, and the body to which the arm belonged. But she *must* do something! She'd call Central and get Gene's number. After that—God knew what!

Her hand trembling so that she very nearly dropped the instrument, she lifted the telephone from the table to the bed. She put the receiver to her ear and after the usual interval at such an hour, when night operators often seem to be sound asleep, she heard Central's weak and far away reply. Nothing stirred in that room of horror except her trembling body and her anguished breathing. So far, her plan was not bringing her lurking enemy from hiding.

She heard the distant ringing of Gene's bell,—ringing, ringing. Again her heart seemed to be in her throat, choking her. Suppose that Gene slept so soundly that no mere telephone bell could arouse him! Many men slept like that. How did she know where Gene had the instrument! It might be in his closet or his bathroom, anywhere but in his bedroom! These possibilities flashed through her tortured brain and made the few seconds seem like hours. Then came a still worse fear. Perhaps Gene had changed his mind and not gone home at all! She remembered that often he had told her of taking long midnight walks in Central Park, when he was unhappy about her and knew that he could not sleep because of her. Perhaps that was where he was, right that moment!

Fear weights time with lead, even when thoughts fly in whirling rapidity through one's brain. Perhaps Central wasn't calling the right number! Her suspense—by this time, acute agony—was unbearable. She signalled for the operator, started to repeat the number, and then—God, the relief! Gene's voice, dull and clouded with sleep, saying "Hello!" as if he'd like to murder somebody if he were not too sleepy to take the trouble.

She almost screamed with the easing of tension. Using what little control she had left, she modulated her voice to a pitch of casual friendliness and unconcern. Her inspiration had come! She knew, suddenly, just what she was going to say to Gene.

"I suppose you'll curse me for waking you up, Gene."

"For Heaven's sake, Margot!"

All sleepiness and latent irritation gone; an eager, naive joy in his tone, struck her as ludicrous, considering her desperate need of him.

"Awfully sorry to disturb you, but I've been trying to read myself to sleep with a French book, and I've struck a passage I can't understand. Will you translate it?"

"Translate—French!" His voice sounded flat with disappointment. Apparently the absurdity of her request did not strike him. Gene was like that—so darn literal. And he was accustomed to her being erratic at all times and seasons.

"Yes. Now listen carefully, Gene! These are the phrases that I don't understand:

"*Il y a un homme au-dessous de mon lit. Venez tout de suite!*"

She pronounced each word with slow distinctness. Her blood tingled in her veins and pricked her skin with the realization that if her enemy happened to know French, it would be all up with her in a few seconds. He might wait until she hung up the receiver, knowing that a sudden outcry of fear from her would give the alarm over the wire, but *after* that—

For an instant Gene was silent, apparently too surprised to answer her. He knew well enough that she read French with ease. Then a laugh came to her over the wires.

"What's the joke, Margot? Surely you know what those phrases mean."

Oh, Heavens! Gene, with his literal mind, and his slow imagination!

"I'll repeat what I said, dear. Guess you didn't hear me."

She had all she could do this time to control the trembling of her voice.

She repeated the foreign words slowly, striving to cut through space to where Gene seemed to exist only as a voice. By the color in her own voice and sheer force of will, she must get her meaning over to him.

Sleepiness perhaps made Gene dense. He translated a little flippantly:

"*There's a man under my bed. Come at once!*"

A third time she repeated the words, then said in English with cautious urgency:

"Get it now, don't you, Gene?"

He got it! She heard his gasp of horror.

"Good God! Be there in five minutes!"

"Wait a second, Gene!"

Another swift thought had come to her. The door to her room was not locked. Thank God for that! She could never have left the bed and gone to the door, even to open it for Gene. She recalled distinctly having put the lock on the catch, early in the evening, and had forgotten to change it. Gene could walk right in!

"Just one more phrase I can't understand. *Pas besoin de frapper. Ma porte est ouverte.*"

"All right, all right. Be right over!"

"Thanks for translating," she said quietly, to complete the pretense, if indeed it were still that. The receiver at Gene's end had already been hung up. "Good night!"

Then—seconds that were years of waiting for *It* to come forth! It would surely come now if her French had been understood. Nothing! Not a sound—not a movement. Only the beating of her own heart, so loud it sounded to her that she wondered if it could not be heard by whatever it was that waited beneath her.

Gone, that particular and immediate danger! *It* had *not* understood French! She relaxed on her pillow with a sigh that was almost a groan of relief. Odd that she should still be safe, she reflected vaguely. Only a few minutes and Gene would be here! Thank Heaven that he lived in the same block! He would have to ring the house bell, but it connected with the basement and could not be heard upstairs. Again thank God for all small mercies.

Hours! Days! Weeks! Then—upon the deathly stillness came a faint sound of creaking wood. Gene was on the stairs! He was on the landing! She could hear the shuffle of his feet! Then—the handle of her door turning without sound, and the next second the door was thrown open, literally hurled back against the wall. She saw Gene standing there, a revolver in his hand. She saw him glance at her as if to be sure of her safety before he could think of anything else. His face was deathly white. Margot lay under the bed covers as stiff and still as if she were dead.

Then she heard Gene's quiet command:

"Get out from under that bed!"

Silence—a silence so thick with suspense that it seemed a part of the living menace which remained invisible.

Good God! Gene was a target as he stood there waiting, his revolver leveled toward the floor.

Margot watched with staring, helpless fear, she too waiting, for Heaven knew what!

Gene advanced slowly into the room, still keeping eyes and revolver pointed to the floor near the bed. Then he spoke again:

"Get out from there if you don't want to get shot!"

Silence, a silence that pressed on Margot's heart like a living thing. She watched Gene take a few more steps closer to the bed. Then suddenly he dropped to his knees, facing the foot-board of the bed, bent until his head almost touched the rug, and aimed the revolver in a quick motion back and forth. Margot could only see the curve of his back over the foot of the bed. She felt she could breathe once more. The fear, for Gene and for herself, had suddenly lifted, for some strange reason.

Gene got quickly to his feet, and stood looking at Margot. His expression of utter amazement would have struck her as comic in a saner moment.

"There's nothing under that bed."

He made the announcement with the calmness of a mind suddenly stunned by surprise and emptied of emotion.

For a second she thought that fear had unbalanced him. Then came a dazed confusion to her own brain. Of course Gene was right! There could be nothing under the bed or it would have attacked him. But—where could the creature have gone—where and how and when, while she lay there watching and waiting in frozen horror?

"I saw a hand—a hand and arm, come out from under the bed, and put out a match on the rug." The mystery which seemed to augment the horror, made her whisper the words.

Gene lifted the small electric lamp to the floor, raised the overhanging coverlet, and looked again under the large brass bed. Then he got to his feet, more slowly this time.

"Nothing there!" His glance at Margot, seeming to raise the doubt as to there having been anything there at any time, made her spring from the bed, oblivious to the fact that she stood before him in her pajamas.

The look she threw him was a challenge and defiant assurance that he was—must be—mistaken. She knew there was something under that bed! She dropped to one knee and stared at the empty space extending to two sides of the wall. Nothing! Absolutely nothing!

She stood up, staring at Gene with a dazed expression, and still innocently unconscious of her attire.

"Something was under that bed! I was wide awake so it wasn't a dream. How could I have *imagined* what I saw!"

"What did you think you saw—I mean, what did you see?" Gene hastily corrected himself.

"I'll tell you what I saw." She shivered in remembrance of creeping horror, and her voice trembled with excitement as she tried to tell him what happened.

"I couldn't sleep, and I lighted a cigarette to take a few more puffs. I dropped the match to the floor, then remembered suddenly the danger on this old rug, I reached over the side of the bed to find the match. Just at that instant a thin white hand and arm crept out, oh so softly and quickly and deliberately tapped the lighted match and put it out, then withdrew back under the bed. *That's* what I *saw,* I tell you, and God knows why I didn't die of fright."

Something in Gene's eyes—a puzzled wonder perhaps— made her say eagerly:

"You look as if you think I'm crazy, Gene. When I called you my life was in danger. Don't you *believe* me?"

"Of course, of course, dear. But it's all right now. Whatever it was you saw isn't there now, and I'm here instead."

His smile was meant to be soothing, but it angered her.

"You're acting as if you thought I were hysterical. I'm *never* hysterical. And I'm not the kind to get any man out of bed in the middle of the night, just on a wild goose chase!"

The tenderness that filled his eyes and his tentative move

toward her, as if to express his tenderness, brought sudden consciousness to Margot of her unclad condition. She was too well bred to apologize or refer to it in words, but she reached to the foot of the bed, seized a silk kimono that lay there, and slipped it on quickly. Then she looked at him almost impersonally, her eyes bright with the keenness of the thought that had come to her.

"Gene! There's a mystery, sure enough, about this room, and we're going to solve it. At least I am, and I'd like to have your help."

Whatever he may have thought about mysteries which brought Margot nearer to him in dependence and trust, he was wise enough to keep to himself. All he said was:

"Righto! I'm keen about detective stuff. You furnish the Sherlock Holmes end of it, Margot, and I'll attend to any scrapping that may form part of the game."

Her face softened and her voice deepened with a throaty note, as always when she was deeply stirred.

"You're *such* a brick, Gene, dear!" Then her lips quivered into a smile which made his heart beat faster. "You're—you're wonderful to me. I don't know what I'd have done without you to-night."

Her eyes filled with sudden tears and she shivered, drawing the kimono closer about her. He took an eager step toward her.

"Margot—darling—you're all in. You've had a fearful nervous shock."

The sympathy in his voice broke down her last reserve. She had poise, and character and a clever brain, but first and last she was feminine and she had been badly frightened.

"You—you don't know what I've been through!" She bent a little toward him as if her own strength were not enough for her.

In the next few minutes, as Margot's head lay against his

shoulder, and dry, nervous sobs shook her slight body, Gene had the sort of struggle that few women understand, to compel his arms to express the tenderness and protective gentleness that was what she wanted of him, and restrain their passionate yearning to crush her against his heart.

Margot understood perfectly. She felt the trembling that went over him like a wave, from head to foot, and she felt his soft kiss on her hair. For the first time she wondered if she didn't love Gene well enough for—well, for marriage and all the rest.

His protective strength gave her back her self-control, and it gave her something else—a realization that it would be good to have Gene's love and strength to depend upon. Still clinging to him with one hand, with the other she rubbed her eyes, then gave a tremulous laugh.

"For an independent female who wants no man's help, I'm doing rather well, don't you think, Gene?"

She looked up into his eyes, and their smile invited his caress. He bent his lips to hers and for the first time since he had loved her, Margot's kiss told him that she cared more for him than any words of hers had admitted.

He kissed her hair, her temple, her throat, just under her ear where her hair swept back. Then he whispered into her ear.

"Darling—you do love me—just a little, don't you?"

"Just a little," she whispered back. As if afraid that she had surrendered too much and too quickly, she drew gently out of his arms, with a glance that told him he mustn't press the advantage gained. Then a frown drew her eyes together, as if to remind him that the situation demanded concentrated thought and action, unrelated to love-making.

"Gene, whether I ever sleep again in this room or not, I've *got* to know what was under my bed and where it went to. You said you'd help me?"

"You bet I will!" His smile was apparently as unemotional as his words.

She stared at the rug where the match had fallen, as if to seek there the first clue in the unraveling of the mystery. Suddenly she ran to the spot, across the few feet of space intervening. She threw herself, literally, to her knees and bent her head close to the rug. Then, excitedly she called to him, without lifting her head.

"Gene! Come here! Look at this!"

He got down on his knees beside her and looked where she pointed. What he saw was a distinct hollow in the nap of the rug, a hollow the size of the tip of a human finger. Into this the black char from the burning match had been pressed and smudged.

Slowly they got to their feet and stood in silence for a few seconds, looked at each other with widened eyes. Gene, for the first time since he had reached the room, looked sincerely puzzled and uncertain.

"I guess that settles it," Margot said slowly. "I wasn't just 'seein' things at night.' Not even a real ghost could have made that mark on the rug. Now, what?"

"Now," Gene said thoughtfully, "with your permission, I'm going to call the police."

She hesitated. Her glance wavered from the spot on the rug, to the telephone, then to Gene.

"I think we'd better. It would be foolish to wait till daylight. Of course they may think us a couple of idiots. Policemen haven't much imagination."

Gene walked to the telephone and called up the police.

"And now, my dear," said Margot, "I've got to put on some clothes before they get here. I'll have to do it here, for I'm scared to go into the bathroom—it might be tenanted." She gave a nervous laugh. "So shut your eyes, old dear, or turn your back, and have your revolver ready in case I have to throw shame to the winds and yell for help."

It took her only a few moments to get into a house dress and comb her ruffled hair. The comb dropped from her hand to the top of the chest of drawers, as a loud banging at the front door resounded through the old house. She stood close to Gene as they listened to the heavy trampling of feet downstairs. Gene ran to the door and flung it open. The officers of the law came up to the landing with a rush, and behind them scurried Mrs. Bellew, in a half-buttoned wrapper and curl papers. For all the excitement and her own nervous tension, Margot's lips twisted with the smile she tried to control as she saw her landlady.

Patrolmen Michael Quinlan and Shane Boyle, stood each of them nearly six feet. Their pugnacious but kindly faces, their clean wholesome skins, suggesting a life spent in the open, their broad blue-coated chests, and their nightsticks, swung with just the right suggestion of authority and force, made Margot's room seem suddenly and incongruously, about the safest place in New York.

Quinlan glanced sharply from Margot to Gene. His voice was as sharp as his words.

"Speak up! What's wrong here?"

Gene, not wishing to dominate the situation, unless Margot wished him to, looked at her enquiringly. She nodded quickly with a smile, then addressed Quinlan, briefly and a little crisply.

"This is *my* room. I occupy it alone." Slight emphasis on the last word. "I'd had a party here. Everybody had gone home and I went to bed. After I'd switched off the electric light, I lighted a cigarette and threw the match on to the floor. It struck me suddenly that it was a dangerous thing to do, so I leaned over the side of the bed to make sure the match wasn't still burning. As I did this, I saw a hand and arm reach out from under the bed—"

"Sneak thief, eh?" Quinlan couldn't wait for the end of her

narrative. "Think he's still around here?" He made a movement to approach the bed, but Margot stopped him with a slight gesture of her hand.

"Wait, please! Let me finish. The hand reached out to the match and tapped the burning end of it. I was too frightened to move or make a sound. Then the hand and arm were drawn back under the bed. I made sure, as soon as I could control my thoughts, that I had a maniac to deal with. I screwed up my courage and switched on the light. Nothing happened, but I fully expected to be murdered any minute. Then I telephoned to my friend Mr. Valery, made up a yarn about wanting him to translate some French I was reading, and got it over to him in French that a man—or something—was under my bed. He came right over in five minutes. When he looked under my bed, there was nothing to be seen."

Painfully conscious, as she neared the end of her story, that it must sound absurd and unconvincing to others, she threw a brightly challenging look from one policeman to the other. Their friendly Irish faces expressed a struggle between doubt of her sanity and amusement at the situation. Then Boyle said bluntly:

"Sounds like a pipe dream to me, lady."

"It's neither a pipe dream nor a nightmare," she said gently. Her common-sense told her that it would be absurd to get up on her dignity because these two unimaginative but kindly disposed policemen, showed frank disbelief of her statements. "Look here, please!" She walked to where the match had been smudged into the rug. "Just bend down and take a good look at that and tell me what you both think of it."

What they both thought of it was not evident in the scowling, bewildered scrutiny they bent upon the rug. Then a thick, red finger went out to touch the spot.

"Don't please!" Margot's sharp command caused the finger to draw back slowly. "We may want to examine that later again," she said more gently. "It must not be touched by anyone."

The officers stood erect and exchanged glances that showed an uncertain state of mind that they were determined to conceal, but Margot's keen eyes saw and understood.

Said Quinlan, squaring his shoulders: "Well, Miss, what do you want us to do?"

"Investigate thoroughly, please." Something in her quiet assurance and dignity went further to convince the two men, that here was something not so easily disposed of as they had thought, stranger than even that queer mark on the rug.

"Sure," Quinlan said, swinging shoulders and nightstick as he approached the bed. "Where's that door lead to?" He indicated the one opening upon the roof-garden.

"There's a roof out there." It was Gene who gave the information. He pointed to another door. "That's a closet, and the bathroom's next to this. Opens into the hall."

Boyle walked to the door opening on the roof, and Quinlan dragged the heavy bed aside, remarking comfortingly to Margot:

"Never a sniff or sign of a living soul'll escape us, Miss, so don't you worry!"

He moved the bed out into the room, then rapped the floor with his stick. There was no cupboard behind the bed, nor any aperture in the wall except a small register protected by a grill through which a mouse could scarcely have passed. He gave a scornful prod to the mattress and struck the bed springs, just by way of not omitting anything. Then he walked to the closet. It was a deep closet and wide, hung with many clothes. It required a few seconds to give the closet its due portion of attention. Quinlan turned back into the room just as Boyle returned from his inspection of the roof and bathroom. Quinlan stood a little awkwardly, swinging his stick. His lips were tight shut in a sort of pursed smile, and he lowered his head a little as he looked at Margot.

"Look here, Miss. Do ye mind telling me what business you're in?"

Slightly taken aback, and throwing a glance at Gene to which he responded by moving closer to her, she said:

"I'm a motion picture actress."

Quinlan lifted his head and the pursed smile widened to good-natured amusement.

"Say! That don't surprise me, at all at all. You movie queens sure like to pull anything to make a story for the papers, don't ye now?" His smile was ingratiating.

For the first time Margot felt angry resentment.

"I've given you my story, told you the absolute truth. I *saw* a hand put out that match. Just because the case is full of mystery is no reason to insult my intelligence."

Quinlan had probably heard of insulting a good many things in the course of his career, but to insult someone's 'intelligence' was a new one on him, evidently. He frowned, then smiled sheepishly.

"Sure, I meant no harm, Miss. Now, just tell me once more, quiet like. You were scared out of your boots, as you might say. Then you phoned this young man." He glanced at Gene. "Now, did you have to get out of bed to let him in?"

"No. The door was unlocked. He walked right in."

"Humph!" Quinlan's brain found this almost too easy. His smile widened. "Sure, don't you see, Miss, didn't it strike you at all, that whoever was under that bed could have crawled to the hall door or the door leadin' to the roof, and made his get-a-way?"

"There was a streak of light from a street lamp, coming through that door." She pointed to the roof-garden exit. "It made a faint shaft of light across the room. I could have seen anything moving over by that door."

"But maybe now, you weren't lookin' in that direction all the time. And it was black, wasn't it, at this end of the room?" Margot nodded. "Well, he could have got to the hall door easy. Too dark to see him, and your heart, likely as not, Miss, was beating too loud for you to *hear* him open and shut the door."

For a moment Margot was staggered by the apparent simplicity of the explanation. Then once more she knew beyond all doubt, that, fear-distraught as she had been during those awful minutes, nevertheless her hearing had been made more acute by her very fear, and she could not have failed to hear the slightest movement in the room. Before she could reply to Quinlan, Mrs. Bellew who had been standing all this time, too overcome by astonishment and fear and Heaven knew what other mixed emotions, to do anything but stare open-mouthed and listen spellbound, suddenly broke forth.

"Oh, my God, my God!" She was almost hysterical from cumulative fear. "That thief or that crazy man or whatever it is, is roaming through my house. I know he is! He's hiding in some empty room. Find him, oh my God, find him!"

Margot went quickly to her distraught landlady and put a hand on her arm.

"Don't get excited," she said gently. "If there's anything—I mean anybody—roaming around in the house, these officers will find him. I'll see to that. So don't you worry, my dear."

Mrs. Bellew's mouth quivered, and tears came into her eyes.

"I'm that nervous," she said tremulously. "What with that girl disappearing the way she did, and that man Murchison, and now this maniac loose in my house, I'm terribly upset, Miss Anstruther."

Quinlan had heard what she said. He went closer to her.

"What's that you said about a girl disappearing and a man?"

Margot, realizing that these other happenings, which might or might not have bearing on her own experience, would only confuse the present issue for Quinlan, said quickly:

"Oh, it's got nothing whatever to do with what happened to me to-night. A girl lodger here some months ago, walked out suddenly and never came back, that's all. And a man living up stairs disappeared at the same time." Her smile at Quinlan was deliberately calculated to mislead him, and it succeeded. He gave a knowing smile and comprehending nod.

"Sure! I get you!" His good-nature was reinforced by the beautiful young lady's confiding manner.

Mrs. Bellew was too self-centered and upset to observe details. She had not caught Margot's smile nor the subtle suggestion in her words, but Gene, delighted at the quick wit of this girl whom he adored, swallowed a laugh with difficulty.

Margot turned more seriously to Quinlan.

"Now, please Officer, search the house thoroughly. But whatever you do, don't leave *this* room unguarded. I swear to you that I saw a hand and arm creep out from under that bed and put out the match. And I *know*—" she raised her hand with a solemn gesture, almost as if taking an oath, "I am as sure as I am that I'm alive, that whatever was under my bed *didn't* get as far as the door."

Quinlan's shrewd look of questioning doubt grew more serious. He turned to Boyle.

"You stick here till I get back. After we're all out, just switch off the light. That'll bring action if there's anything round this neighborhood. Here, give me a hand with the bed."

They shoved the bed back into place, then Quinlan, again swinging his stick and his shoulders, went to the hall door.

"Come on, you people. Better find somewheres else to

sleep till mornin', Miss Anstrooter." He got the name out with difficulty.

Margot, Gene and Mrs. Bellew went downstairs and waited in the dimly lighted front hall. From time to time they caught the chittering voices of lodgers who were being disturbed by Quinlan's search. Finally he joined them below, remarking that he had still to take a look at the front and back parlors. He struck the parlor door with his stick. The blow against the heavy wood resounded in the silent house.

"Not but what he'd have ducked for the street, right off, and—"

His sentence was never completed. A roar of sheer terror thundered through the house. Mrs. Bellew gave a scream, and Margot seized Gene's arm.

"Mother Mary!" Quinlan almost whispered the words, and his eyes bulged.

The door of Margot's room, which could be seen from the foot of the stairs, burst open, and Boyle dashed down the stairs, face ghastly white and eyes staring. He seemed oblivious of the four figures in the hall, and made a spring for the front door. Quinlan threw out his arm and caught him.

"For the love of God, what's eatin' ye?"

"The hand! The hand!" Boyle was beyond lucid speech.

"*What* hand?" Quinlan shook him and shouted at him.

"The hand from under the bed!"

"You saw it too?" Margot seized Boyle's arm with trembling fingers. Her flesh was cold and tingling.

Boyle crossed himself. He spoke in a choked undertone.

"Standin' there—in the dark—the Holy Saints take witness—it came out—from under the bed—and doused a flame on the rug!"

CHAPTER IV

MOUNTING MYSTERY

Dawn streaked the eastern sky with orange and gold. A crispness in the air made Margot draw her cape closer about her. She and Gene had spent the intervening hour in Mrs. Bellew's basement room, and now they stood on her own roof-garden, reveling in fresh air after the stuffy atmosphere below, and watching the beauty of the dawn through an open space between two houses to the east of them.

Margot had more than a stuffy atmosphere to get rid of. She wanted, for a brief moment, to shake off the memory of nerve-racking hours, first in the room with the creature of the hand and arm, and, since Boyle's sensational climax, the bored depression of listening patiently to Mrs. Bellew's wailings, and warnings of still more trouble to come. The landlady could conceive of no human agency in the appearance of the ghostly hand and arm. No speculation as to human motives or mystery were of interest to her. The only explanation that seemed to fit the case for Mrs. Bellew, was a spiritual one. In plain simple vernacular, the house was "haunted," and would continue to be haunted, therefore bad luck would attend it and her. She had a ten-year lease and the law would not release her because of ghostly visitations. It was equally certain that no tenants would remain with her once the truth should become known.

Margot had always been interested in psychic phenomena, and was too open-minded to be skeptical as regards any psychic manifestation. But in this instance she stuck to her belief that the amazing hand belonged to the body of a living—a sinister—human criminal.

Quinlan and Boyle were at this moment prowling heavily about Margot's room, and wrangling as to whether anyone had seen anything come out from under the bed. They had reported to the station house by telephone, after Boyle had steadied his shaken nerves, and had been ordered to remain where they were and get to the bottom of the matter if possible.

Margot turned from the narrowed but close view of the East River, glistening in the first sunrays of early morning, and motioned to Gene to listen to the policemen inside the room.

"Listen to them, Gene! They're awfully amusing."

Argument and rehearsal of the night's drama, ended each time with something like this:

"The young lady maybe was dreaming, as you say, Quinlan, and maybe she *wasn't* dreaming. All *I* know about it is that *I* seen it with me mortal—me wakin'—eyes,—a thin, white hand it was,—the hand of a ghost, God have mercy on us!"

"Ghosts!" Margot gave a low chuckle as she heard the disgust and scorn in Quinlan's voice. "Ghosts, is it? Ain't ye ashamed to have such a heathen thought!"

"Heathen, am I? Well, tell me this, if ye're so smart ye are! The young lady saw a hand put out a match she had dropped on the floor. The light she saw was a match burning. Get that don't ye? How about the flame of light I seen with me own eyes? It wasn't a match, I'll tell ye that, for I hadn't lighted no match, and that ye know as well as I do."

Quinlan's reply was a grunt that scorned further argument. Margot's smile faded as she turned serious eyes to Gene.

"That's just it, Gene! Even that ignorant man in there, sees something there that can't be explained by ordinary theories. That's what would make almost any intelligent person feel sure that the mystery has a psychic meaning. But nevertheless, I'm sure it's something else."

"See here, Margot darling. Don't be angry with me if I say— what it's easier to say in the cold light of morning—that you *may* have had a sort of waking dream—a realistic staging of your imagination which fooled you into thinking that—well, that it wasn't your imagination at all. I happen to know that such things have occurred even to unimaginative persons."

"All right, old dear, granted, for the sake of argument." Her smile accepted his skepticism without the resentment she had felt a few hours before. "And granting that, of course it's quite simple to explain what Boyle experienced as the fevered imagination of a superstitious Irishman. But there still remains the smudge on the rug. You can't suppose that I got out of bed, terrorized as I was, before you got there, and it is certain that neither of us made that mark *after* your arrival."

"Dearest, that match might have fallen there before you went to bed, and been stepped on by you, unobserved."

"Now, see here, Gene! I know that 'evening thoughts grow cold at night,' to quote some philosopher, or, to paraphrase him, midnight thoughts freeze up entirely before daylight. Before you called the police you were ready to concede that I wasn't *imagining* things. And you agreed to help me get to the bottom of what I consider a mystery—a human mystery, not a psychic one. Now, are you going back on your offer?"

"Absolutely not! I'll do anything you want, and not express a doubt to anyone."

"Righto! Then stop expressing them to me, from now on. And now let's go out and rustle some breakfast. After I've braced up with some strong coffee I'll come back here and dress to go to the studio."

"And by the way," she added, "if you get to the shop before me, don't you breathe a word to anyone! It's *my* story and I want the fun of telling it."

When Margot returned to her room a half hour later, she found Quinlan a trifle dubious about leaving her alone in the room. She told him that she had to dress for the day—bathe, etc.—and asked them to wait on the landing, if they absolutely wouldn't go down stairs.

Daylight—sunlight—made of her room so cheerful and normal, even so commonplace a setting—so absurd a setting for mystery and mystic marauders—that she laughed at the notion of keeping two policemen there all day on guard. Of course there was nothing queer or inimical lurking about now in broad daylight! Time enough to watch the room after nightfall.

She felt weary, utterly let down, now that the excitement of her midnight adventure had abated. Young as she was, and pretty, she could not afford to go to the studio looking fagged, with unbecoming shadows beneath the eyes and the iris clouded from lack of sleep. A hot tub, a cold shower, setting-up exercises, and a moderate disposal of rouge and powder over her clear skin, and she was ready for the fray. Instinctively she always half expected it to be some sort of a fray with Stoner as director and would-be lover.

Arriving at Astoria about nine o'clock, she hurried to the

main production floor. Her big scene in *A Toreador's Love,* was to be shot to-day, she remembered, with a faint thrill of antici-pation. She couldn't possibly, in the present circumstances, feel more than a mild thrill over anything unrelated to the mystery she was so eager to unravel. However—it behooved her to forget it for a while, charm Stoner if need be, and certainly to fulfill the promise she had shown in previous scenes of making good in her big scene.

Tall scenic creations—the sides of buildings, garden walls embowered in greenery, the prows of ships—were jumbled together, leaned against each other in stacks. The place suggested that mysterious region behind the curtain, stage and backstage, of many opera houses thrown into one fantastic whole. Carpenters and mechanics hammered and hauled. In the midst of the confu-sion, here and there, were completed sets where scenes were being shot; rooms furnished to the last detail, with only one or two walls apiece, rooms where actors strolled and mimed, and upon which blazed the batteries of assembled Kleig lights.

Margot knew that the movies have a doctrine of efficiency to which they seldom adhere. Promptness was an unwritten law, but when you were told to be on hand at nine o'clock sharp for the filming of a scene prepared the day before, if you were in costume by eleven it would be too early because the cast would probably have luncheon before settling down to work. The amount of time wasted throughout the day was truly remark-able. Margot knew her set was not even ready, and that the instructions given her to be on time were little more than an official gesture.

However—might as well be ready! She changed her clothes then picked her way through the tangle of props to where May Cheshire, Lulu Leinster and other girls were chatting. They were all in their street clothes, Margot observed with a smile.

Through the slats of a cabin on wheels—Corinne Delamar's dressing-room—shone electric lights indicating that the star was "making-up." Frederick Stoner, for once, lounged silently, while the stage hands adjusted a Spanish balcony. What was the matter with Stoner, Margot wondered, with amused indifference! She had never before seen him so restfully quiescent—restful for all the rest of them.

A quick glance at the incurious faces of the girls assured her that Gene had kept silent as to what had happened. But of course Gene would, even if he hadn't promised her to do so. Gene, who had maneuvered to be the camera man on this particular job, stood apart from the crowd, tinkering with his camera. His back was turned to her. Margot had a sudden impulse to go up and speak to him. It would be incautious, perhaps, to indicate the very faintest friendly interest in Gene while they were in the shop. It might irritate Stoner but—to perdition with Stoner! She'd do what she wanted to, such a little thing anyway. And Gene was *such* a brick!

She approached him with a gentle:

"Hello, Gene!"

He swung around at the sound of her voice, almost dropping what he held in his hand. His eager eyes swept her from head to foot. He hadn't seen her in this Spanish rig before.

"By the Lord, Margot, you're stunning! Beautiful Andalusian, except for that glimpse of your hair." He lowered his voice to a whisper. "You're as fresh and lovely as if you hadn't been up all night."

"All depends, you know, what you're about, when you're up all night. They say that when you're keenly interested in something or somebody, you don't show fatigue, and you'll have to admit that I was keenly interested in *something—and somebody!*" She laughed, looking at him out of the corners of her roguish eyes.

"I suppose you're endowing a myth—an apparition—with personality," he said a little somberly.

"Take care!" She shook a finger at him. "You promised not to express the least doubt in future, even to me. But, as a matter of fact, old dear, when I used the word 'somebody,' I really *meant* you."

The sudden light in his eyes warned her that it was no place in which to play with fire, the fire being in Gene's eyes. She whispered that she'd see him later in the day, and turned to join the other girls. Just then Stoner saw her. He stood only a few feet away, but he approached nearer, where she stood next to Lulu Leinster.

"Hello!" he greeted her, appraising her with his quick, shrewd eyes. "Top of the morning! Sleep well, after that grand little party of yours?"

"Not a wink!" Her bright glance was friendly enough, but she did not smile. She often gave the impression of smiling when actually her mobile lips remained closed.

"What on earth—" he began, sincerely mystified. "You don't mean that the mild drinks and our milder society, made you as wakeful as all that?"

"Oh no, I don't mean that!" Her smile was vaguely irritating to him. "I didn't sleep a wink because I was rehearsing the first scene in New York's greatest detective mystery."

For a second his eyes narrowed, or she thought they did, and seemed to probe back of her words. Then his expression changed swiftly to an amused understanding of her light mood. A mere jest, of course, he seemed to say with the smile on his full lips.

He stepped a little closer to her, but did not raise his voice.

"Trying to call attention to your youth and beauty by pretending that they're proof even against a sleepless night?

You don't need to, my dear." His bold glance was like an unwel-come caress.

The unexpected twist he had given her remark, annoyed her, and his glance was an affront.

"Nothing of the sort! I *was* awake all night, and it *did* concern a mystery."

Again he studied her, a little puzzled.

"Guess it would take a good live mystery to keep *you* awake, Margot. You couldn't work yourself up to such a pitch just by telling or listening to a tale like the one you gave us about that girl who disappeared, and the old fellow."

She had almost forgotten the story about Stella Ball and the man Murchison. Odd, too, because she recalled that when Mrs. Bellew had nearly gone into hysterics when the policemen were examining the room, it had struck her as remotely possible that there might be a connection between the old and the new mystery. Now, she felt suddenly, with a little shudder, that it might be more than remotely possible.

"You've said it, Mr. Stoner! That's just what it was and is—'a good, live mystery.' And something new to fact and fiction. A creature without a body or a face. It was in my room for hours."

The other girls were crowding around her, pushing and buzzing like a swarm of insects. She smiled at one and the other, then, with another glance at the director, she said calmly:

"A policeman saw it, too!"

In the midst of the chirping and excited cries of the girls, she distinguished Stoner's low exclamation of astonishment.

"A policeman! What on earth were you doing with a policeman?"

"Nothing wrong, I trust." She could not resist the facetious retort, nor control the smile of amusement that almost broke into a laugh at Stoner's angry dignity. The girls, at least, had the sense to giggle, but that only made Stoner more indignant.

"See here, my dear young friend, I've got a busy day ahead of me, and so have you. Can't waste time with foolish cracks. You made a statement regarding a policeman. Was that your little joke?"

"No it wasn't!" she snapped, her eyes suddenly flashing. Stoner annoyed her. "Something darn queer happened last night—*so* darn queer, that I called Gene Valery on the phone, because, frankly, I was frightened out of my wits, then we called the police."

Open-mouthed and speechless interest greeted her on the part of the girls, and a few men standing by now, on the edge of the circle around her. To her surprise, Stoner also was silent, watching her intently out of half-closed eyes. She gave them the story from beginning to end, repeating the high spots for the emotional avidity of the May and Lulu types of mind. She hardly expected very intelligent or constructive comment from any of them, but Stoner's first remark surprised her. She had counted on him for a bit of racy skepticism. But he said, with a dark frown:

"Rotten thing to have happened—rotten!"

"Why rotten?" Her sense of irritation with him increased. "I may have to wait a long time for another such break in the monotony of my life."

"Should think you'd rather have some other kind of diversion than a low-down burglar sneaking in and out of your room at night."

"Who said it was a burglar?" Again she snapped at him. "Nothing so commonplace as that, I assure you, or I shouldn't have taken the trouble to talk about it." She caught Gene's eyes over the heads of the excited girls. He had approached and stood outside the circle. She addressed him directly.

"I'd call it an extraordinary mystery, wouldn't you, Gene?"

"Decidedly extraordinary," he said quietly.

Stoner's quick glance at Gene warned her that she might dare much in personal encounters with the director, but that for Gene's sake and her own, she must be more cautious where he was concerned. She contrived to smile more pleasantly at Stoner.

"Yes, it's a mystery, and what's more, *I'm going* to solve it!"

"Want to be a female Sherlock Holmes, eh?" he said sullenly. "Well, I'd advise you not to. There's danger, meddling with that sort of thing."

Something in his tone and manner warned the girls that their director would prefer to talk alone with Margot. They faded away regretfully, their curiosity by no means sated. The men strolled off and Margot found herself facing Stoner's eyes in which there lurked, or she fancied it, a faint menace—the menace of a will opposed to her own. She took up the gauntlet.

"What do you mean by danger, Mr. Stoner?"

"Danger of your melodramatic story breaking into the newspapers."

"I don't understand," she frowned at him. "What if it did? I'm neither a society bud nor a sister of mercy. I am—or trying to be—a motion picture actress. If publicity ever hurt any woman in *this* profession, it's news to me." Her smile was a little mocking.

"See here, Margot!" He threw off suddenly his aggressive manner. "You know I've done all I could to give you a chance,— shove you ahead. I've no object in giving you a wrong lead. When I advise you to lay off of freakish publicity, it's only for your own good."

Mollified, but still dubious and puzzled, she said:

"But I'm not planning to do *anything* just for the sake of a write-up. My investigation of my little mystery is going to be dead serious. If the papers get hold of it and send reporters to me, I'll give them a straight story. What's wrong about that? They make up what you don't tell them, anyway."

Stoner seemed to hesitate, then he said quietly:

"I see I've got to be frank with you, Margot. You're not a star *yet*, my dear girl, and you can't afford to pull front page stuff that would make the leading lady sore."

Taken by surprise, Margot stared at him.

"You mean—Corinne Delamar?"

"Think she'd like to see *you* head-lined, when *she* hasn't been able to make the papers in a big way since we started this picture?"

"Why—I hadn't thought of her at all."

"Well, girlie, you've got a think coming. She'd be sore as hell, take it from me. I know her."

"Of course," Margot began doubtfully, "I don't wish to antagonize Miss Delamar. But how do you know she wouldn't get interested herself, if she knew what a strange experience I've had! Suppose I tell her about it?"

"No! Drop the whole business—please!" Stoner's face was flushed and there was sharp command in his voice.

More annoyed with him than she had ever been before, Margot flashed angry rebellion at him, then she turned away with brusque indifference to appearances, walked off the floor and went upstairs to the dressing room she shared with a few other girls.

She was more than annoyed at Stoner's unsympathetic attitude, and what struck her as an attempt to bully her. The more she pondered the matter, the more puzzled she grew. If he were sincere in his stand regarding publicity, why had he vacillated in argument? First he had warned her against the harm of freakish notoriety, then he had switched to the possibility of arousing the star's hostility.

Suddenly the absurdity of it all struck her—her own absurdity above all, for it *was* ridiculous of her to have taken Stoner so seriously, and not seen below the surface to his real motive. The simple truth, so she felt, was that Stoner was indulging unreasoning and petty jealousy of Gene. He hated the thought that Gene and not himself had been associated with her in an adventure. He hated still more the idea of this association becoming public news. She recalled his glum demeanor when she had told of Gene coming to her supposed rescue. Obviously, Stoner would go far to prevent a sensational sequel to the adventure, which would bracket her name with that of the man whom he regarded as an impudent rival. It would be most galling to a man of Stoner's character.

Finally she resolved that nothing should induce her to discuss the matter in the studio again that day—or any other day, for that matter! And she stuck to her decision in the face of a regular bombardment of feminine questions. Stoner was less easy to avoid. He had more approaches than one. He led her aside about an hour after she had reappeared on the set. His first remark was so blunt and apparently sincere, that it took her off guard.

"So you won't credit me with being in love for the first time in my life?"

Her stare of surprise was as frank as his question.

"Why—really," she stalled, with a faint smile. "I never consider such things in working hours."

"Be serious!" he commanded frowning. "You'd better understand, first as last, that we're both in a game where love and work are often mixed up, pretty close sometimes."

She loathed him for his implication of favoritism at a price. With a cool little smile, she said:

"I've told you several times, Mr. Stoner, that I'm not the least interested in the game of love, just at present, with you or any other man. I mean what I say. Why insist?"

"Because I want to get it well into your head that I really am seriously in love with you. I'd like you to believe in me, even if you can't love me—yet. Now, take that question of my advice about publicity. You acted as if you thought I was trying to injure you."

"Oh, no," she said sweetly. "I'm quite willing to acknowledge your good intentions." She could not control the touch of sarcasm in her smile. But he seemed not to notice it, which was as well.

He grew more cheerful. His smile was ingratiating.

"I've been thinking that it mightn't do any harm to make a cautious investigation of your spook. Suppose we go over it together. Have dinner with me, then, afterwards, we could look through your quarters for clues."

"I'm sorry, Mr. Stoner, and thank you very much, but I have an engagement to-night."

His face clouded instantly. "As usual," he growled.

She passed that up, then said gently:

"Even if I could dine with you, to-night, Mr. Stoner, my mystery wouldn't form part of your entertainment. Second thoughts are not always best. Not in this case anyway. You told me emphatically to drop my mystery—not investigate it. And that's that!"

They stood looking at each other, Margot serene and smiling, Stoner scowling and affronted. Then, her eyes, with their uncanny power to detect thought or emotion in other eyes superficially inexpressive, witnessed for the third time since she had first met him, that strange dilating of the small pupil; that queer overtone as of a yellowish shadow darkening the pale blue of the iris; that shimmer in the eyeball, like dust specks seen in a sunbeam. She had once more that sensation of hearing something she could not understand; something that he was unconscious of saying.

Then Stoner walked away, and Margot stood motionless, with an intangible, vague wonder in her groping mind.

Hours later, Margot, standing on the side lines, dressed as *Conchita,* felt no surprise that her director had so manipulated matters during the balance of the day, that her scene was not called. As she watched the filming of secondary shots, she felt relief that her first important scene had been postponed. She was in no mood to do herself credit, and she was glad that Stoner's petty resentment had given her such a good chance to rest and wait. If he had intended to make her regret her treatment of him, how disappointed he would be, if he knew the truth.

Suddenly she was aware of Corinne Delamar's rather arrogant stare from across the lot. A scene had just been finished, and the star stood at ease, smoking a cigarette. For the moment Stoner was busy and unobservant. Margot stared back, but without impudence. It was rather as if she said to Corinne: Well, sorry you don't like me. Suppose you tell me why!

The unspoken challenge reached perhaps to the brain of Miss Delamar. Deliberately and slowly she crossed to where Margot stood. She went close to her before she spoke. Then she said:

"I want to talk with you, Miss Anstruther. Will you come to my dressing-room?"

Surprised, but not averse to an encounter—she felt vaguely that it would be that—with the star, Margot smiled her willingness to follow Corinne to her dressing-room. A couple of uncomfortable chairs, two cigarettes, a slight pause over the ponderous matter of lighting them, and then:

"What's your little game?" drawled Corinne, lazily puffing and inhaling and blowing smoke through her small nose.

Margot, with a gasp and the flashing thought that never would she learn to cope with women of the star's type, said gently:

"I'm sorry if I'm stupid, Miss Delamar, but I'm afraid I don't understand what you mean."

"Oh—*don't* you?"

Vague suggestion of insolence made the blood mount swiftly in Margot's face. It showed through her make-up.

"Frankly, I don't," she repeated gently. "I might imagine many things, but I prefer not to,"

"Well, I'd hate to have you overwork your imagination, so I'll help you out. Are you playing Frederick Stoner just on general business principles, or is it something more—personal?"

Quick resentment flamed into Margot's gray eyes, but she controlled herself to say gently:

"Will you tell me what right you have, Miss Delamar, to assume that I'm 'paying'—as you call it—the director, from any motive "whatsoever?"

"Don't be ridiculous, please! Try to talk as if you gave me credit for having at *least* as much intelligence as yourself."

Margot half rose from her chair, on the impulse to leave Corinne forthwith, not condescending to give her a reply, rude or courteous. But another impulse followed and held her in her chair. For some reason too vague to analyze, she wanted to conciliate Corinne, if this could be done without loss of dignity.

"Miss Delamar, please try to believe me when I tell you that I am *not* making use of the director, either for professional purposes or personal ones. I've tried, of course, to be friendly with him. Who doesn't? I'm quite sure that a girl can't expect to get very far in pictures, without favoritism or some sort of pull or backing, unless maybe she has extraordinary talent."

"Tell me—which of us two—you or I—has 'extraordinary talent'?" Corinne's pretty lips twisted in a smile of malice and irony.

Margot detested flattery, but she caught the implication in Corinne's question—unexpectedly clever of Corinne!—and realized that she was treading on thin ice. Corinne was a violent little thing. Better not arouse her.

"Well, I'm fairly sure *I* haven't got extraordinary talent, nevertheless I have hopes of getting on without influence, so I'll modify what I said. A girl *may* get on if she's fairly good-looking, screens well, can act pretty well, and has a personality that helps to get her over."

Corinne gave her a grudging smile.

"You're smarter than I thought you were. You've summed up things flatteringly for both of us. I have all the assets you mention, so that lets *me* out. No suggestion that *I've* had any favoritism to boost me. And it lets you out too! Miss Anstruther, if I didn't dislike you so much, I could almost find it in my heart to love you." Her smile was not unamiable.

Frankly surprised, Margot said quickly:

"Why do you dislike me so much? I know you've avoided me, and I know that you think I've flirted with Stoner and—and—all that," she fumbled with slight confusion, remembering the ridicule in the remarks of girls who had told her that the star was jealous of her and Stoner.

"Well, I'll take your word for it. I kind of thought I saw signs of your having come over into my yard to play—when I haven't been around. Understand, my dear? But if you say you've just kind of wandered in by mistake, and if you'll agree to sort of leave my—my yard alone, why I guess I won't hate you."

If Corinne had used the word "property" instead of "yard," her meaning could not have been clearer, Margot reflected, with eyes lowered to conceal her reflection. She rose and tried to smile cordially.

"I hope that you and I will be friends before this picture's finished. I admire Mr. Stoner for his ability and for his jolly good nature which doesn't often get spoiled. But, frankly, Miss Delamar, he isn't at all my type, nor am I his. He's interested, of course, in the talent he believes I have, but naturally—and *obviously*—he's far more interested in *your* talent."

That ended the strange little interview, but not Margot's reflections upon it. Late that afternoon Gene contrived hurriedly to make an appointment with her for dinner. They left the studio separately and met in New York at a specified restaurant. Afterwards they went to what Margot facetiously called the house of mystery.

CHAPTER V

WEIRD SUSPICIONS

During dinner Gene had made several attempts to swing Margot into a mood which would be at least gracious to his love-making, but she had been distrait, which was more disconcerting than a frank rebuff. On the way home he held her arm with a pressure that evoked only a light laugh.

"Funny old dear," she said teasingly. "You're determined to be amorous to-night, but really, Gene, I can't take my mind off my mystery, even for a minute. Do you know, I haven't telephoned home all day, just because I didn't want to take the edge off my return. Let's hurry and see if there have been any new developments."

Gene followed her lead, but took a silent oath to kiss her before the evening should be over, mystery or no mystery.

Once over the threshold of the house on Forty-ninth Street, they felt at once the atmosphere of suspicion and jangled nerves, as embodied in the person of Mrs. Bellew. In Margot's room they found Quinlan and Boyle, both on guard, with the landlady hovering about, babbling theories that no one was interested in.

The policemen told Margot that a plainclothes detective from headquarters had been there to interview her, and would shortly return. A few minutes later he appeared, a cold, shrewd officer, who answered to the top-heavy name of Cornelius Hart. He seemed like an intelligent type, but intolerant. Evidently he had brushed aside all second-hand reports, insisting upon getting Margot's story from her own lips.

For the fourth time she gave her narrative without embellishments. Hart listened attentively and prodded her with occasional questions. Finally he said:

"Miss Anstruther, I think you have a powerful imagination."

It was what she might have expected, but she felt the same unreasoning resentment which all skepticism regarding her experience seemed to evoke. She said quietly:

"This policeman," she glanced at Boyle, "saw what I saw."

"Sure! Boyle's an Irishman. He'll see anything anybody else sees. They believe in the Banshee, where *he* comes from."

Boyle growled an indignant but indistinguishable protest.

"Many mysterious happenings which have been explained in the end, have appeared just as fantastic in the beginning as what I've told you." Margot tried logic on Hart, without success.

"The chief difficulty, Miss Anstruther, in accepting the arm and hand you describe, is that they were attached to no body."

"How do you *know* that?" she came back at him quickly.

"Well, looks that way, doesn't it?"

"All right, let it go at that, but don't you think it's a problem worth at least *trying* to solve, that an arm *apparently* attached to no body, nevertheless did certain definite things? Put it that way."

Hart shrugged his thin shoulders. He glanced around the room.

"This place has been searched thoroughly, and more than once. There are no traces of anyone having hidden under the bed."

"How about the hollow in the nap of the rug where a finger-tip pressed down the match?"

"Maybe. It's fluffed out now. I can only say that there isn't the slightest evidence that a crime was committed or attempted. So it doesn't seem to concern the police department."

Margot regarded him with serious eyes. He was as cold and impersonal as a fish.

"Then you are finished with the case?"

"Not quite. Sleep somewhere else to-night. I'll leave Quinlan to watch this room. If there's nothing to report by to-morrow, we'll be through."

Hart left, and Boyle, heaving a great sigh of relief, went with him. Margot asked Quinlan to wait downstairs for a half hour, as she had something to talk over with her friend. She went down with the policeman and asked Mrs. Bellew's permission for him to remain in her sitting-room. Quinlan's expression of despair at the prospect of half an hour of uninterrupted conversation with the landlady was comic. But Mrs. Bellew smiled happily at the prospect, oblivious of Quinlan's unflattering scowl.

Alone with Gene in the brightly lighted room, Margot threw herself with a sigh of relief, on the divan. She let him sit beside her, but she refused even to let him hold her hand.

"Gene, old dear, my brain's on the rampage. I haven't an emotion to-night capable of sitting up and taking notice of the love-making of a veritable Valentino." She laughed and patted his hand. "But I do need your sympathy and advice—dreadfully."

"I have a vision of you taking my *advice*."

"Well—perhaps that isn't exactly what I mean, but I want to talk things over with you,—get a few trifles off my mind."

She told him of Stoner's peculiar behavior and comments on hearing of her ghostly adventure. She repeated laughingly his warnings about Corinne Delamar, but she omitted his avowals of devotion, and his anger because she had refused to dine with him that night. It would be unwise to give Gene any additional reason for suspicion and jealousy of Stoner. She decided to refrain even from telling Gene of her conclusions as to the director's motives for begging her to drop the matter of the mystery. Gene would be enraged at the bare idea of Stoner having the impudence to be jealous where Margot was concerned. And as to his motives,—she had begun to wonder if her conclusions hadn't carried her far afield of the truth. That was just what she wanted to discuss with Gene—Stoner's *motive* in being apparently so upset about her having publicity.

"Do you know," she ended her recountal with a fixed stare across the room; "at times I feel as if there were something queer about Stoner—something vaguely sinister and disturbing. At other times I laugh at myself for such an idea, especially when he's in one of his boyish, boisterous and entirely simple-minded moods."

"What first gave you such an idea about Stoner? He seems to me the crudest, most obvious type of male."

"I guess it's his eyes—mostly." Margot's own eyes looked full of the enchantment of mystery. "They certainly have a weird expression at times."

"What do you mean by 'weird'? The way he looks at *you?*"

She smiled at Gene's quickly aroused suspicion and resentment.

"No, it's nothing personal. That's the odd thing about it. There are moments when he looks at me but doesn't really see me for a second. And his eyes seem to be saying something that he's unconscious of saying and that I can't understand. It's happened more than once."

Gene's adoring smile was then a little quizzical.

"That's a little trick of yours, Margot, darling, to read things in eyes that are really quite without expression."

"That's where you're all wrong, old dear," she said quickly. "Often when a person's eyes look positively blank to others, they tell *me* something in total contradiction to what their lips are saying. It's most embarrassing at times."

"When did you first notice this *weird* expression in Stoner's eyes?" Gene looked as if Stoner as a subject for conversation might be improved upon.

"Oh," she said eagerly, "that reminds me. I've never told you about the day I first went to the Superfilm studio for a job. Maybe after I've told you certain things, you may be clever enough to throw light on Stoner's pale eyes."

She laughed at Gene's exclamation of disgust, and began her narrative.

She told him of her embarrassed entry into the waiting-room of the casting director, when she had run the gauntlet of rows of feminine eyes—eyes of the other girls on the same errand as herself, and waiting in various degrees of irritation and boredom. She laughed in amused reminiscence.

"Every head in the room bobbed—including my own. Just a difference in color and cut. Lipsticks, powder-pads, tiny mirrors—rows of them. And their poor, pathetic little faces, Gene. Vacuous smiles on carefully painted lips, and hardened eyes that should have been young and weren't. And pair after pair of flesh-colored silk stockings—mine were tan that day, and I was glad of it. And their attenuated skirts adjusted modestly an inch or two above the knee. I wanted to scream with laughter, but suddenly I wanted to cry, they were so pathetic."

Gene interrupted her with a quick pressure of her hand.

"Just like you, Margot. Your sense of humor gets a good fillip out of something, then suddenly your desire to be helpful comes uppermost."

"Oh, it wasn't that. Don't sentimentalize about me, Gene. It was only that I felt that those girls, with their stereotyped prettiness and vacuous vanity, probably needed work and money, far more than I did. Then I laughed at myself realizing that they'd stand a better chance of getting it in that place than I would. Then, my dear, we all got a shock. Lulu Leinster, with that wonderful little head and body of hers, walked into the room. *Her* hair *wasn't* bobbed, and it was glorious, hanging in two huge braids. Primitive hair, hurled at one's vision that way, was provocative—almost indecent." Margot laughed again, and stroked her own shorn locks.

"It's a wonder, with your excessive modesty, that you didn't depart at once, leaving Lulu without a competitor." Gene teased her with his broad grin.

"My dear, that's *just* what I was on the point of doing, while Sam, Stoner's bodyguard, was flinging his questions at her, and she coolly informed him that she'd been sent by a beauty contest committee in Texas, she having won the prize. Then, before I knew it, Sam stood in front of *me*, asking the same fool questions. The next thing I knew, every girl in the room, except Lulu and me, was marching out, having been told by Sam that they needn't wait. He was so suave I wanted to kick him. And the girls filed out, tossing their heads and clicking their heels, and curling their angry lips. A few minutes later Sam ushered us into Stoner's august presence."

Margot interrupted her story to let Gene light a cigarette for her. She took a few abstracted puffs, the smoke winding slowly upward from her parted lips, then she told Gene how the director stood by his desk, frowning at the two girls as they entered his sanctum. How he then sat before his desk and addressed himself first to Lulu, asking her name and address. How he disposed of Lulu and turned to Margot with the same questions. Margot's eyes darkened with excitement as she stressed this part of her narrative.

"I gave him my name, then my address. The minute I said 809 East Forty-ninth Street, Stoner's head jerked up, and his light blue eyes looked straight into mine. He repeated the number of the house—not the street—and his face was impassive, but suddenly I noticed his eyes. The pupil dilated, and a sort of yellowish shadow darkened the iris. I caught a strange shimmer in the eyeball, like dust specks seen in a sunbeam. Of course I may have imagined it all, but that was the very first time when I seemed to dread something in his eyes that confused and mystified me."

Gene studied her reflectively. "What did he say after that?"

"Oh, he looked down at his desk, then up again at me, quickly, then he remarked that I must have one foot in the East River. His eyes were as blank as pale blue eyes can be, even in an intelligent head. I told him that it was an easy step down, but not quite over. Then he stood up and calmly told us that they only needed one more girl and that he couldn't decide which of us would screen the best without a test. He told us to come back the following day. And oh, Gene, I never told you what Lulu said to me." Margot chuckled in gleeful remembrance. "When we parted in New York she announced that she'd probably not see me again. For a second I didn't get it. I looked my surprise, then she said: 'Why—er—you ain't going back there to-morrow?' Then I understood, and I asked her why not. She got a bit rattled and said that she didn't suppose I'd want to go to the bother. I smiled and remarked that it wouldn't be any more bother for me than for her. She had the grace to stumble as she said: 'Maybe my funny face is more what they want than yours.' I remarked that that fine point remained to be proved, and that perhaps we'd *both* be chosen and become rival stars. Poor little Lulu is short on humor. She didn't see the joke. Anyway, we met in the studio next day, and now, my dear Gene, I've come to the really interesting part of my story."

"Tell me first, Margot, if you got the impression from the way Stoner looked at you, that he admired you personally?"

"Oh," Margot shrugged indifferently. "I don't suppose he regarded me as a piece of bric-a-brac, but what I mean had nothing to do with me as a woman or an actress. Of course the impression faded and I felt, afterwards, that I'd been over psychic or suspicious, as usual. But that night the impression returned stronger than before. It even made me hesitate about going back."

Margot told of being escorted by Sam—together with Lulu— to the stage where a close-up of some scene was being registered. Margot had seen interest flash in Stoner's eyes when he saw the two girls waiting to be noticed by him. He had chucked Lulu under the chin but had refrained from a like playful greeting with Margot after one glance into her eyes.

He had again asked her name, then he had said:

"So you live on Forty-ninth Street, in one of those ramshackle houses built before the flood? What did you say the number was?"

Margot had told him.

"What floor do you live on?"

"For a second," said Margot, "I thought he meant to be impudent, but I decided he meant nothing offensive, so I told him that I lived on the first floor. Then he asked if my room was front or back. I had another impulse to glare at him, but instead, I said politely that I had the large room in the rear, and added that he seemed to know the house. It was then that I thought I caught that queer glint in his eyes again, and a slight challenge in his glance. He said indifferently that a friend of his had lived in this house and that he hadn't seen it for years. He remarked that I must find the place uncomfortable and inconvenient. I told him I didn't. Then he announced that he would make a test of Lulu first."

The two girls had been directed to put on make-up, and when they had appeared properly mascaraed and powdered, he had indicated a place for Lulu to stand. He had told her, with a good-natured grin, to think hard of her "sweetie," and to imagine she was meeting him by the light of the moon, and that he was going to take her in his arms and hug her. Lulu had smiled in full understanding and self-assurance and had proceeded to spoil her beauty by a forced and absurd expression of rapturous parted lips. Stoner had groaned.

"Oh, Lord, that won't do! Think again, not so hard, maybe. Relax! Try to feel what you'd really feel if the fellow you love stood right in my boots!" Stoner had laughed boisterously at his little joke.

That time Lulu had done much better. Margot, watching her, had decided that Lulu had the making of a good movie actress—above the average—and this impression was followed by the humble assurance that she would certainly not register as well in this silly test as the little beauty-contest girl, whose egoism was of so different a variety. If Stoner had needed two girls, perhaps she Could have passed muster, but not in competition with Lulu.

"Then," Margot went on with a laugh, "I heard Stoner calling me. I remembered what I'd been asked when I was a kid:—which would I prefer, be a greater fool than I looked, or look a greater fool than I be. I knew I'd explode if he invoked the figure of an absent lover. But Stoner isn't a fool. He took me by surprise by telling me to imagine that I'd just seen—was still looking at—something that froze my blood with horror. Somebody run over or murdered. Or, better still, I must register the emotion that would overcome me if I were alone in the dark, and suddenly saw something that didn't belong there—something spooky, with an agonized face, calling for mercy. Wasn't it uncanny, his striking that note of fear and horror, considering what happened so soon afterwards?"

"Yes, it was," agreed Gene quickly. "You don't need to tell me how you registered those faked emotions. The results speak for themselves. He selected *you* instead of Lulu."

Margot leaned forward excitedly, and put her hand on Gene's arm.

"That's just the odd part of the whole performance—something I've never told you before, Gene. As to how I registered, I guess I didn't do badly. Either Stoner's surprising eloquence or the memory of a ghost story heard years ago, that had made my blood run cold—literally—or whatever it was, my imagination took fire and I actually saw before me, for that moment, the thing of horror. Funny, but I never thought of that odd coincidence until to-day. Well, Lulu told me afterwards that my eyes dilated, and my lips quivered. In short I 'registered,' and Stoner gave an expression of approval. Then he looked from Lulu to me, and finally he said:

"'You're all right!'" He shifted his gaze back to Lulu, and said: "'So are you, girlie. Damned if I know which of you is the best. Have to wait and see the proofs. Come back to-morrow morning or stick around now for a few hours.'"

"Of course we told him we'd return the next day. Lulu's rapturous smile seemed to indicate that she was sure of what the proofs would show. We started to leave and at the far end of the stage, within a few feet of the entrance, we heard Stoner's stentorian call, asking us to go back a minute. He was whispering to Sam and one of the camera men. Then he came up to us and said:

"'I've decided not to wait for those pictures. 'Tisn't necessary. I can tell just from looking at you two, which one is the best— the best, anyway, for *my* purposes.'"

"I felt Lulu tremble with excitement. I thought I saw again that faint glitter in Stoner's pale eyes. Then, looking at me he said:

"'It's you I want, Miss Anstruther. Come back to-morrow to start work. The part you'll get isn't a small one. It'll mean work.'"

Margot told Gene of poor little Lulu's sobbing disappointment, and of Stoner's attempt to console her by advising her not to be soft, and not to mind, as it was all in the game, and it was a hard, hard world anyway. He had ended by saying that he had chosen Margot because she suited the part in the picture, better than Lulu. He had been speaking to Lulu, but Margot had caught his gaze fixed upon herself. Intuition told her that he had chosen her for personal reasons. She had registered fairly well, but so had Lulu, and Lulu was decidedly more the screen type of beauty, with her fine profile and wonderful hair.

"You see, Gene," Margot summed up eagerly, "my first conclusion was that I'd made a strong appeal to Stoner. Perhaps I saw that much in his eyes, but there was something else in his eyes. It eluded and mocked me, but it was there—something that was neither admiration nor desire. I felt half inclined to refuse his offer, when I heard him telling Lulu that since she was so unhappy, he'd fix her up. There was a girl on the lot who needed a rest. He'd give her a vacation on full pay and Lulu could have her part in *A Toreador's Love*. Only the part of a lady's maid, but if Lulu wanted it—etc., etc. And then he said to me—while Lulu was washing her face, that he hoped we'd be friends, and that he hoped I'd let him call on me some evening soon."

Margot could not resist a dramatic pause, just to give Gene a chance to frown in angry indignation. He did not disappoint her.

"Damn nerve! What did you tell him?"

"Well, I was on the point of giving him a sharp retort, when he said, casually:

"'What was that number again? 809 East 49th Street?'

"Once again I was arrested by the look in his eyes—that strange yellowish shadow covering the blue of the iris, and the dilating of the pupil. That's all, Gene, but I'd like to know what you make of it?"

Gene looked puzzled and uncertain. "You mean—why he chose you instead of Lulu Leinster?"

"Yes, of course, that's what I mean."

"Search *me,* Margot. You make it all sound very mysterious, and you draw a picture of old fat Stoner that's far more interesting and thrilling than anything he can ever hope to be in the flesh."

"Perhaps you think my imagination's gone wild along with my brain. No, old dear. Just think hard, a minute. Don't you honestly think it rather strange—in all the circumstances— that he should have chosen me? And remember all I've told you about his eyes, especially in connection with my living in this house!"

Gene threw back his head with a jerk of sudden astonishment.

"You think Stoner's connected in some way—in the past— with this house—with what's happened here?" Gene's blue eyes were troubled and mystified.

"Well," said Margot slowly, "I'm not *sure* of anything, and it's too soon to draw any definite conclusions about Stoner or anything else, but I do feel that in some way that I can't fathom, Stoner has a personal reason for wanting me to drop the investigation of my little mystery."

Gene pondered that a moment, then he said abruptly:

"Can't get it at all, Margot. I'm convinced that all those weird expressions you've been seeing in Stoner's eyes, can be boiled down to just one thing—his mad admiration for you, my dear girl."

Margot jumped to her feet, and seized Gene's hand with a laugh.

"That's about enough from you for one night, old silly. I'm tired out anyway, and poor Quinlan's half hour has stretched out till I dare say he's ready to kill me. So off with you, Gene! See you to-morrow, and here's hoping you'll have done some heavy thinking in the meantime!"

She let him kiss her good-night, then she ran down stairs to tell Quinlan that he could return to his official duties.

CHAPTER VI

THE MIDNIGHT PROWLER

Margot was to sleep on a cot in Mrs. Bellew's basement. She made a rite of brushing her thick reddish hair, and invariably let her mind wander while she did it. Mrs. Bellew's chatter had the effect of dripping water. It made her sleepy, and she was horribly tired. Some sixth sense told her that sleep was not for her that night; that the mystery would soon take a new and fantastic turn.

With bored disgust she discovered that she had forgotten to bring down her pyjamas. She started for the stairs, then turned back into the basement room. She told Mrs. Bellew that she didn't want to go up to her room alone. No reason whatever, Quinlan being so decent, but she felt nervous, and would Mrs. Bellew mind going up with her? Mrs. Bellew cheerfully assured her that she didn't mind at all.

They climbed the stairs and knocked lightly on the door. Quinlan let them in and they stood for a moment with him in the dark. Margot, her voice instinctively pitched very low, explained her errand. Then she whispered to Quinlan:

"Seen or heard anything?"

"No, Miss." Quinlan's was a veritable, stage whisper.

Suddenly he stiffened and threw his arm out to bar Margot's way, as she started in the direction of her closet.

"Shh!" he admonished tensely.

Margot stood stock still, as she heard Mrs. Bellew's stifled cry of fear. They heard a faint scraping sound. It seemed to come from the roof-garden, the door leading to which was open a few inches. Quinlan had left it so. Then, the shadow of a human being fell slantwise on the curtain over the door, and loomed large against the rift of light from the street lamp. Faint creaking of the door pushing inward; a figure, indistinct, crouching uncertainly; then upright, stepping more boldly into the room, and moving slowly toward them.

Mrs. Bellew's terror broke in a shriek. Quinlan lunged forward and seized the intruder. Margot dashed for the switch-button in the wall, and flooded the room with light.

A girl stood there, her shoulders pinioned from behind by Quinlan's big hands; a girl with white, drawn face; a black-browed, sullen young creature, who uttered no sound of fear or pain. Too astonished to move or speak, Margot stared. Then another shriek resounded in the room.

"It's Stella—Stella Ball!" Mrs. Bellew managed to gasp the words.

Margot trembled with excitement. Her breath came short.

"The girl who lived in this room?"

"Herself—oh, my God!" The landlady was on the verge of frenzied hysteria.

Margot swung fiercely about to the girl.

"Tell us what it all means!" she commanded sternly.

"I'll tell you nothing!" The retort was almost vicious in its quick intensity.

"We'll make you talk quick enough," growled Quinlan.

"I haven't committed any crime." She made the assertion unwhiningly. "You can't do anything to me!"

"I arrest you for unlawful entry, with intent to commit a burglary. Guess that'll do for the present."

The girl's lips clamped stubbornly. There was a touch of pride in her defiance. Margot was conscious of it, and sudden pity gave her the impulse to ask Quinlan to release the girl. Her connection with the mystery seemed remote indeed, if not highly improbable. Her coming was merely coincidental. Then—

Margot's glance fell to the girl's right arm. The grip of Quinlan's fingers had pulled the sleeve up. The arm had been cut off at the elbow! Margot's gaping eyes saw the scar of a freshly healed wound. It made a grim patch of color against the white of her arm.

Mrs. Bellew's frightened eyes went from Stella Ball's blanched face to the stub of her right arm. A horrified, fixed stare, then a third shriek from the landlady. "My God! She had both arms when she left this house!"

Stella's thin little face lost its expressionless rigidity. She smiled; a strange, twisted ghost of a smile, on one side of her mouth, yet it had humor, that smile, humor wasted of course on Mrs. Bellew, but startling to Margot.

"Hell of a lot you know how I looked when I left your shanty. Didn't happen to see me light out, did you?"

Mrs. Bellew was too far overcome with nervous excitement to have any other emotion, so she did not resent the girl's impudence. Margot, watching intently, saw the smile on Stella's face vanish as quickly as it had appeared. Her face hardened again, her lips grew tight with a bitterness in tragic contrast to the youth of her face, as she looked at the lurid scar which had riveted Margot's attention. Then she gave an angry hitch to her right shoulder, twisting her sleeve out of Quinlan's grip, so that it fell over and covered her disfigured arm.

"Let go of her, please, Mr. Quinlan!" Margot's quick command was spoken gently enough, but Quinlan removed his hands from Stella's thin shoulders.

Being momentarily deprived of action, Quinlan found release for his tongue. He stood with arms crossed, regarding the girl with an angry scowl.

"Think ye're smart, don't ye now, disturbin' honest folks, and scarin' this nice young lady out of a year's growth and raisin' hell generally, just to do a little stealin' where there ain't nothin' to steal, far as I can make out."

The girl flashed a defiant look at him.

"Who says I came to steal?"

"*I* says it, for one!" Quinlan gave her look for look. "Your kind—or any other kind—don't come sneakin' in other people's windows and doors, just for their health. They come to get something—that's what they come for—or maybe," he bent a threatening scowl upon her, "maybe they come to murder somebody."

Mrs. Bellew gave a low cry and shuddered closer to Margot.

"Ain't you the smart Alec!" Stella's twisted smile at Quinlan was not flattering. "Maybe I did come to get something. This used to be my room. Maybe I came to get something I left behind, when I beat it on such short notice." Her smile of mockery went from the policeman to the landlady.

"I took all your things down stairs, Stella. I'll give them to you."

"Didn't have to sneak back to get what belongs to ye. There's a front door to this house, if ye know how to use it." Quinlan's sarcasm was a little heavy. He was no match for the girl, Margot thought, amused in spite of all that the scene evoked and might well signify.

"Front doors are good 'nough for some people—the kind that wouldn't dare come in any other way. 'Fraid for their precious skins, maybe."

"Say, look a-here, Miss Smartie! If you'd come back on the level, to get your belongin's, why didn't ye tell this young lady so, when ye found the room was occupied?"

"Saa-y!" The girl's sweeping scorn of Quinlan, was comic. "Hell of a chance you gave me to tell anybody anything, grabbing me with those dainty mitts of yours, in the pitch dark, before you saw who or what I was!"

"I'm not talkin' about your little stunt to-night, comin' in from that roof, and gettin' caught redhanded, I might say. I'm talkin' about night before last when ye honored this young lady with a call and pretty near frightened her to death."

Stella's eyes opened and stared in a surprise that struck Margot as strangely genuine.

"Don't know what you're trying to celebrate, Mr. Officer-of-the-Law. This is the first time I've come to this room since I left it when I was living here. I wasn't in this room night before last."

It was Quinlan's turn to retaliate with a scorn as scathing as her own.

"No, you wasn't here night before last! Yes, we have no bananas! I—don't—*think!*"

"I wasn't! Think what you damn please!" A flash of anger quickened the tired lifelessness of Stella's blue eyes.

Quinlan moved a step nearer to her, and thrust his head out at her.

"You wasn't hidin' under that brass bed, for the Lord knows how long before Miss Anstruther went to bed, and you didn't stick your hand and arm out from under the bed and put a burnin' match out, after the young lady had switched off her electric light?"

The surprise in Stella's eyes changed slowly to astonish-ment, then another, more subtle change came to them. Margot, with active brain and unwavering, watchful gaze, and uncanny power to read back of the human eye, saw in Stella's Something that she could not analyze, but something that convinced her as no words could have done, that the girl was telling the truth and that Quinlan's remarks had quickened a wondering specu-lation in her mind, concerning something of sinister import to Margot's mystery.

"I wasn't in this room night before last. Take that or leave it! I should worry!"

Sudden inspiration came to Quinlan.

"Then if ye wasn't here yerself, ye know damn well who *was* here!" Intuition or reason, whichever it was, Margot thought, Quinlan was less "dumb" than he had appeared up to now.

Stella threw him a startled, questioning look, then her lips grew sullen and her eyes hard.

"Let's get a move on," she said laconically. "Don't suppose you want to entertain me here for the night. Ain't you just bursting to show me your hospitality somewheres else?"

"See here, Miss Stella Ball, if that's yer name. Suppose ye spill a little information about the friend of yours that hid under Miss Anstruther's bed the other night. Give us the dope—the real dope and all of it, and we'll see what we can do about lettin' ye off with a minimum sentence, maybe none at all."

"I've got nothing to say about anything, because I don't know nothing about nothing! See?" Stella gave Quinlan another of her twisted smiles, touched with an ironic humor.

"Won't save yerself by squealin', is that it?" Quinlan's naturally good-humored mouth had a more kindly expression.

"No, that ain't it!" Her reply was as enigmatic as it was brief and final.

They could get nothing more out of her. She remained stubbornly silent, her face reverting to its original hard blankness. Quinlan told her she'd have to go with him, arrested on the charge of unlawful entry. Then he turned to Margot, with the air of being the Heaven-sent sleuth and unraveler of mysteries which the case had so urgently required.

"Guess you can come right back to this room and have a good night's sleep, Miss Anstruther. Guess no more spooks is goin' to disturb your rest, from now on. There'll be those as'll know how to get the truth out of this girl, to-night or to-morrow. Guess ye're safe enough now."

"Wait a minute, Mr. Quinlan." Margot addressed the policeman but her eyes were on Stella Ball. "You seem to be sure that either this girl or some confederate of hers, was under my bed night before last, and put out the match I dropped on the rug. But how about the hand and arm that Boyle saw, when *he* was alone in this room, putting out a light that didn't even exist?"

Margot saw a quickly suppressed shudder, a swift lifting then closing of lids over startled blue eyes, then stillness on the impassive face of Stella Ball. Quinlan saw nothing. He was busy preparing a reply to Margot's question.

"It's a friend I am of Shane Boyle's, Miss Anstruther, but it's only tellin' the truth I am, when I say that Boyle bein' born in the auld country, and comin' here when he was full grown, is as full of superstition as a dog is full of flees. It stands to reason, Miss, that whoever it was put the match out when you lay in that brass bed, wasn't doin' the self-same thing for Boyle's benefit, because whoever it was, got out of this room before ever any of the rest of us set foot in it. That's as sure as that I'm standin' on me two feet this very minute. So it stands to reason, don't it, that what Boyle saw, came out of the square Irish head on him."

"Do you think so, Mr. Quinlan?" Again she spoke to Quinlan but looked at Stella.

"Sure, I think so. What else could I think?"

At Margot's simple question, Stella again lifted heavy lids and dropped them as quickly. In her tired blue eyes Margot caught a vague question and challenge directed at herself. Then Quinlan departed with his prisoner.

CHAPTER VII

SPOOKS AND THE PRESS

Margot and Mrs. Bellew returned to the basement for the night, locking Margot's room on the outside. Another sleepless night would play the mischief with her looks, but Margot found sleep an impossibility. She wished she could call Gene and tell him what had happened since he left the house, but she decided to wait until the following day.

With tired brain and thoughts spinning around as actively in sleep as when awake, and far more fatiguingly so, Margot had about three hours of unconsciousness. Then, as on the previous morning, a hot tub, a cold shower, setting-up exercises, a little make-up, and she looked, even if she didn't feel, as good as new, she decided, after careful scrutiny of her face.

She decided to be late to the studio, and move all her belongings from the room she had occupied, to one which Mrs. Bellew had offered her, on the floor above. The landlady and her housemaid helped Margot in the process of moving up the one flight. She said that for the present, she would take with her only her personal effects. It was best, she told Mrs. Bellew, to leave the room intact, in case any further inspection should be deemed advisable by the police department. Therefore she did not remove her rugs, nor hangings, nor other articles of room adornment, which belonged to her. She rather expected to hear further from the police before the morning was over, she told the landlady.

About ten o'clock, the plainclothes man Hart arrived, asked Margot a few superfluous questions, then gave his orders that Margot's room—the room of the bodiless hand from under the bed—was to be turned over to the police department. A man from the Force was to be left there, day and night, and the key would be kept by the police. Hart assured Margot that although theft was probably the motive for the midnight visitation— granted that there had been any such appearance as she had described—he was sure that criminal intent to do bodily injury was not involved, and as to anything of a supernatural nature, that was of course ridiculous.

It struck Margot as ridiculous that the police should occupy her old room as a field for research in a case which they insisted was neither criminal nor supernatural. But she refrained from telling Hart what she thought about it.

Before she left the house at one o'clock, already two reporters and three news photographers had made their unwelcome appearance. It was evident that the rest of the day would bring other relays of the inquisitive pests. She was glad to escape, leaving poor, harassed Mrs. Bellew to do the honors. Of course the garrulous landlady would talk of things she knew not, and say many things that the newspaper men would twist to suit themselves, but Margot knew that it mattered very little what was or was not made public in the way of news regarding her adventure. The publicity itself was the one inescapable fact.

The morning papers had had nothing regarding the affair, so there was as yet no need to dread an encounter with Stoner. She had decided not to tell Gene, should she meet him at the studio, of Stella Ball's unexpected re-appearance, until the evening.

On her arrival at Astoria, keyed to make excuses for her late arrival, and to remind Stoner of her fruitless and long hours of waiting the day before, Margot found that the screening of *A Toreador's Love* was held up for a few days, possibly for a week. Some blunder on the part of the art director. The set had to be revamped. It was one of the frequent movie comedies of errors, which they had all learned to take philosophically. All but Stoner, who was in a condition of blasphemous wrath. He must indeed be upset, Margot delightedly observed, not even to notice her late arrival.

Corinne Delamar darted acid comments through the slats of her dressing-room on wheels. The minor members of the cast had been told to get out of the way. The girls she knew crowded around Margot, asking if she had seen her spook the night before, and if that was why she was so late at the studio. To all questions she smiled and said that she believed her ghost was laid, that she had seen nothing weird the previous night, and that she was late to the studio, merely because she was tired from her previous adventure.

As a matter of policy and precaution, she hung around the studio until late in the afternoon, then disappeared before the other girls were ready to leave. Gene did not go with her, but in a hurried interview between them it had been arranged for him to come for her later and take her out for dinner.

The first thing she did on arrival in New York, was to buy an evening paper. The headlines of the early edition greeted her; headlines about herself; bantering, hateful headlines:

SPOOKS PURSUE FILM BEAUTY—ACTRESS AND COP GET GHOSTLY BURGLAR—MOVIE GIRL REPORTS ROOM HAUNTED.

Well—she had known what to expect. But at least she could put a check on the melodramatic absurdity of it all. She wished to goodness she had stayed at home that day and talked with all the reporters herself. Trust foolish Mrs. Bellew to make things as absolutely ridiculous as possible! She hurried home, called up the leading newspapers, and requested that they send special men to interview her that evening. It would, she believed, ensure a more rational version of the story, at least.

Dining with Gene, she gave him a detailed description of what had occurred the night before, but she omitted all comment as to her impressions or deductions. She wasn't ready yet to go into all that. Later in the evening, after she had interviewed the newspaper men, she would take Gene fully into her confidence.

He disapproved of her remaining in the same house. Why on earth did she want to do that? he asked her.

"Well," she said, with one of her cryptic smiles, "I have my reasons, old dear. They may be foolish ones, time will tell, but in the meantime, I've made up my mind to stay right in that house of mystery."

"All right, my dear. I always respect the results of your mental processes, but sometimes the processes themselves leave me in the air."

"A very comfortable place for the present, Gene. You may wish you'd stayed up in that safe region, before we get through with this thing."

"Not unless you were up there with me," he smiled back at her.

Later in the evening, after Margot had flattered and flustered and successfully maneuvered the newspaper men, and had given each one a cocktail with which to drink to her success as a star in filmdom and as a detective in her field of mystery, she and Gene settled down in her new room to a serious talk.

"As I see it," she summed up, "this mystery is a perfectly normal one. It's my firm belief that it will turn out to be more important to students of crime than to the Society for Psychical Research. Moreover, the best detective methods are the only methods that will solve it."

"Meaning—Cornelius Hart and his hot-on-the-trail assistants?" His smile expressed the scorn he shared with her as regards the plainclothes man.

"Absurd bungler, isn't he? First he laughed at my story, and ridiculed Boyle. Then he woke up when Stella came on the screen, but he can't get a word out of her. She's much too clever for him. And his investigations in this house consist of watching for something new to happen, which isn't *going* to happen. The dub isn't using what brain he happens to have."

"What's your idea? To go to one of the private agencies and get one of their men? The trouble is the price, dear. They charge at least twenty dollars a day."

"No, nothing like that." She laughed and struck her chest with a comic gesture. "Little one, you see before you the real Sherlock Holmes in the plot! *I* am going to apply to the case the expert methods I referred to. And of course you're going to help me."

"Righto!" He smiled, then grew more serious. "All very fine, Margot, but for all your cleverness and powers of analysis, I don't quite see what you've got to go on."

"Don't you! Well, now listen. Get down to bedrock and to essentials. I saw an apparently unattached arm. The next night Stella Ball sneaked into my room. Stella Ball has comparatively recently had her right arm amputated at the elbow. I believe that these three strange, apparently unrelated facts, are actually, if mysteriously, related."

Gene couldn't control a slight shudder.

"Isn't that going back to the spook theory you said you'd rejected? Surely you don't mean, Margot, that you think it was a psychic manifestation of some sort,—the girl sending her arm ahead of her, or something of that sort? You can't be serious!"

"Not that way, no. That's too absurd! But let me go on. For some reason the hand I actually saw—for keep in mind that I *did* see A HAND!—found it important to put out lights on the floor. Stella Ball had lived in that same room. For all we know, she might, in the past, have penetrated its secret. Last night she may have come either to help or to thwart that hand."

"What do you mean? In putting out the lights on the rug?" Gene was making a valiant effort to treat Margot's theories with the respect she demanded.

"Not necessarily. I'm trying to stick to logic. It's always so easy to regard a sequence of odd occurrences as mere coincidence. Gene, think me a fool if you like, but I'm dead sure that the hand had a living owner. I'm very nearly as sure that Stella and the owner of the hand were after something in that room of which they both have knowledge."

"Oh! Then you don't think the hand you saw belonged to the girl?"

"No, I don't. Of course I have no theory as yet as to *what* they were after. The flames on the carpet will probably prove to have a lot to do with it. So will the fact of Stella being armless."

"Gosh!" Gene heaved a sigh of despair. "Frankly, Margot, you've got me out of my depth. Look here! Granted that you and then Boyle saw a human hand and arm, how do you explain the way it vanished both times? Wouldn't it argue a hiding place for the body belonging to the arm?"

Margot's face glowed with enthusiasm. She put out an eager hand and squeezed Gene's.

"Bully for you! You've struck the nail on the head! Of course, it argues just that."

"But, good Lord, the place has been searched thoroughly, It's the one little thing the police have done. You can't think anything's been overlooked?"

"Naturally I think it. If you've ever dropped your collar button, Gene, you must realize that looking in vain for it twenty times doesn't prove that you only imagined you had the collar button."

Her sense of humor was indestructible, and Gene smiled, but his own humor expressed itself with a note of sarcasm.

"Suppose the intruder might have hidden between the spring and mattress of your bed?"

Her merry laugh was incongruous with the sense of mystery that increased with everything she said.

"Quinlan took that idea quite seriously, if you remember. Nothing living or dead could have lived through the pounding he gave the bed with his nightstick."

"Do be serious, dear. How about the fireplace?"

"Serious! And you make a suggestion like that!" She laughed again. "Naturally not the fireplace. It's several feet from the bed. If the creature could have reached the fireplace without my hearing or seeing it, then it could have got to the door just as easily."

"Oh, I give it up!" Gene lighted a cigarette with the air of seeking consolation where he could reasonably hope to find it.

"Well, I don't—not by a good deal. I don't *know* anything. What I'm really doing, Gene, is to follow the Sherlock Holmes method of discarding the alternatives that are obviously impossible."

He looked at her sharply. "You mean—there remains an alternative—an escape—which doesn't strike you as impossible?"

"Yes."

Gene got quickly to his feet. "Come on," he said eagerly, seizing her by the hand. "Show it to me!"

"Go easy, Gene! We mustn't tamper with a thing. It's best to direct the police what to do. But we can take a look, if we can make some excuse to get that policeman out of the room for a little while. I'm not keen on taking *him*, into my confidence." She got up and moved to the door, still speaking: "You see, the *object of* Stella's return to that room is what I want to—"

She was interrupted by a sharp rap on the door. Cool as Margot looked and felt, she gave a slight start, then she stood back to let Gene open the door. A messenger boy stood there holding out a yellow envelope, and piping "Telegram!"

While Gene signed for her, and shut the door after the departing boy, Margot tore open the message. Then she handed it to Gene. Her gray eyes looked troubled and her mouth drooped at the corners.

"What do you make out of this?"

Gene read it aloud, in a slow, puzzled fashion.

"See me at the studio to-morrow morning without fail.

"CORINNE DELAMAR."

"It looks as if what you said Stoner told you about her high-and-mightiness was correct. She's probably furious because you've broken into the papers. What other reason could she have for sending you such a message?"

"That's it, of course, but I'll bet Stoner put her up to it. I had a feeling when he talked to me, that he was inventing the thing for some purpose of his own. She isn't a bad sort, you know. I don't believe she'd have dreamed of being jealous of me if someone hadn't put her up to it. Well, it can't be helped. I'll sleep on it. We'll have to postpone our detective work. I must be clear-eyed and clear-brained to tackle Delamar in the morning."

Her good-night kiss to Gene was hardly what his lover's desire could be satisfied with. He held her for a moment, whispering of his love for her, but he knew her well enough to realize that until Margot should have disposed of Corinne Delamar, and Stoner and a few other details such as the mystery of the hand and arm, he could expect little response to his passion. Wisely he let it go at that.

That night Margot dreamed—a strangely vivid dream—not of Stella Ball, nor of the mystic hand and arm, nor of Corinne Delamar, still less of Gene whom she had begun to love. She dreamed (and awoke from the dream, trembling and longing to cry out, as one feels on awaking from a nightmare) of Stoner; not Stoner attempting to force his coarse passion upon her; not Stoner enraged at her for disobeying his orders to drop all probing into the mystery of her room; but Stoner, looking at her as he had looked that first day when she had given him her address, looking at her with pupils dilated, the overtone as of a yellowish shadow darkening his pale blue eyes; the shimmer in the eyeball like dust-specks in a sunbeam!

Wide awake, she shivered and lay thinking for hours . . . thinking. . . .

CHAPTER VIII

THE CLAWS OF JEALOUSY

Margot arrived at Astoria at about ten o'clock on the following morning. She raised clear eyes to the zenith, praising, whatever it was she was accustomed to praise deep in her soul, that the sky in its blue immensity was there above her, promising unseen glorious things beyond her ken. Mere joy of living made her face sparkle in response to the sparkle of the sun, and she took in deep breaths of tingling air, which quickened the flow of blood in her young body, and brought a brighter color to her cheeks.

Probably the one precious gift of the gods which should have meant more to her than beauty or vigor or quick wits, was the one on which she placed the least value, taking it for granted, as those who are very young invariably regard the short-lived possession of *youth*. In spite of three successive sleepless nights, much excitement and considerable nerve strain, youth had refreshed itself from unguessed sources. No one would have imagined, to look at Margot, that she had anything more weighty to consider than whatever immediate and trivial objective might lie before her.

Nevertheless she was conscious of an increasing annoyance as she approached the studio. The impertinence of Corinne Delamar's imperative dispatch, created an irritation which was close to angry indignation by the time she entered the big edifice. A sudden decision not to appear too hasty in her response to the star's command, made her take a roundabout way to the dressing-room which she shared with other girls.

A confusion of props and other scenic paraphernalia, stood about near the stairway leading up to the girls' dressing-room. The place seemed momentarily deserted. She heard hammering and voices over at the end of the vast stage, but at the end near the stairway there appeared to be no one.

With one foot on the bottom step, she heard a slight sound that arrested her. Deliberately she stood still and listened. The sound referred to was the use of her own name in the voice of Miss Delamar, and the voice came from the other side of a large piece of scenery which completely cut off the view of the stairs. Margot had no idea what Corinne had said about her; she heard only her name, but forthwith she determined to know what further the star intended to say about her. The old saying about listeners, might well apply in this case, but Margot felt that in all the circumstances—and the fact that she felt an instinctive mistrust of Stoner—she was justified in using whatever self-defensive weapons chance might offer her.

Then she heard a man's voice—in a second she recognized it as Stoner's—saying:

"Don't let her put anything over on you. She'll have her own story to tell, of course, but just you stick to the main fact—the only one that cuts any ice with you—that being that she's got herself in the limelight just when you need all you can damn well, get for yourself."

"What do you want me to say to her? The harm's done. She's been headlined in all the papers. That *can't* be undone." Corinne sounded a little querulous.

"You can raise merry hell with her, can't you? Make her sorry she didn't put the lid on tight to this idiotic mystery stuff, as I warned her to. Make her sorry she's alive, if you have to. Sorry so far as her job here is concerned, or any other job in pictures. Between us we could queer her with any other company." Stoner's voice was rasping with irritability.

A slight pause, then Corinne said:

"You've got a bee in my bonnet and you're determined to make it keep on buzzing. If you hadn't put it into my head, I'd never have thought that Margot Anstruther having a mysterious adventure which has got into the papers, could have a thing to do with *my* getting press publicity. As a matter of fact, why haven't you seen to it yourself, Fred?"

"Good Lord, I've done every damn thing I can to push you, my dear girl, and you know it."

Strangely familiar words, Margot thought with a smile.

"I'll tell you flat what I *do* know!" Corinne's rather light voice vibrated with sudden feeling. "You're more interested in that girl than you're willing to admit. Don't think me a fool, my dear Fred. Both my eyes and ears are normal, and I've seen and heard things."

Margot heard Stoner's low laugh of amused contempt.

"Oh, you women! The girl's got talent of course, and the artist I flatter myself I am, recognized it and made use of it. Why not, will you tell me? All women have to be flattered to get good results, whether it's work or play." His laugh was teasing, patronizing. "But as to my feeling any deeply *personal* interest in Miss Anstruther, why you're a fool to imagine it for a moment."

"Of course, my dear Fred, don't get away with the idea that I would make any fuss or try to force an issue with you, where there isn't one. I mean this. It's been no question of marriage between you and me. I'd bow to the woman who could inspire you to want to get married. But—and it's a big one—I'll not stand for your having an affair with Margot Anstruther or any other girl, and let things go on as before between you and me, no matter how much I happen to be indebted to you for being a star so early in the game."

"Laying down the law, is that it, my dear?"

"Yes, that's precisely it. If you can get that girl to take my place to your complete satisfaction—in or out of marriage—why go to it, old dear, but count me out—not only of your personal life but out of your picture."

"You're not such a fool as to threaten to quit work on this picture in the middle of it, just out of jealous spite over another woman?" He had raised his voice and it vibrated angrily.

"No, you big nut, I don't mean that. I'm not going to cut off my nose to spite my face just out of jealousy, but I'll do it in a jiffy if there's real foundation for that jealousy."

"You mean, if you found out that I'm interested in Margot Anstruther—let's say, for the sake of argument, in love with her—you'd leave me and my big picture high and dry, and I'd have to begin the thing all over again with another actress?"

"Exactly!" Corinne's voice was crisp and cool. "And I have a sweet picture, dear Freddie, of what you'd hear from the Superfilm production manager when he would find out that your infatuation for a new girl cost the company thousands of dollars."

"You little devil!" There was nothing jocular in the remark. "Well, now listen to *me!* If I really cared a damn about this girl

Margot, I'd see you or any other woman in Jericho, before I'd be threatened or dictated to. But if it'll smooth your feathers to know the truth, here it is, little one. Personally, Margot means nothing to me. I'm interested in her work, and I've got a certain curiosity about this mystery story of hers. Detective stuff *always* interests me. So if you see me talking to her, you can be sure it's either about work in the studio or about her ghosts. But as to this publicity stunt, we've got to choke it off, and I depend on you, Corinne, to do what you can with her. Give her a scare, and see what *that'll* do."

The tone of finality in Stoner's long-winded speech, made Margot run lightly away from the staircase. The interview between Corinne and Stoner was probably ended, and the quicker Margot got out of the danger zone, the better. She hurried back to the front entrance, and came sauntering in, again walking directly to the end of the stage where work was going on. She had a vague plan to encounter the director first, see what he might have to say, then go on to the interview with the star.

Funny, Stoner telling Corinne that he liked detective mysteries! Just the opposite of what he'd told Margot.

Coming around the corner of a chrome yellow plaster wall of a Spanish farmhouse, she almost ran into Stoner. He stared, then bent over her, with a surly expression.

"You would do it, wouldn't you! You *would* be written up, in spite of what I told you!"

Margot smiled, an enigmatic smile that brought an angry flush to Stoner's face. Then she said quietly:

"Don't you think that the initiative was taken out of my hands by the arrival upon the scene of the mysterious girl, Stella Ball?"

"That's got nothing to do with what I mean, Miss Anstruther. You gave interviews to the reporters, didn't you?"

"Naturally. They got hold of the story from the police, and they published a lot of bunk that I went to some pains to contradict. You'll find a much more sane story in to-day's papers."

"Makes it all the worse. If you'd let the whole thing drop as a silly pipe dream, after that first night, and sent the police packing, *nothing* would have got into the papers."

"O—h!" Margot opened wide her large gray eyes. "You wish I'd taken possession of my room as if nothing had happened, and been all alone to receive and entertain Stella Ball on her informal visit to my quarters?"

"How could *she* have hurt you, a thin little thing like that?"

"Thin little thing, like that," Margot repeated, staring at him.

For a second something flashed in his eyes, or she imagined it, then he frowned and said testily:

"Well, that's the way the papers described her, wasn't it?"

"Oh—yes, of course, I forgot!"

Surely her thoughts were taking erratic twists and turns. Why had she been struck by an undefined familiarity with the appearance of the girl Stella, in Stoner's casual comment? A vague impression, going as quickly as it had come, and leaving her with the sense of being somehow a trifle foolish.

"Can't see," Stoner went on with the argument, "what there'd have been particularly scary about having a girl sneak thief come into your room. You don't strike me as a coward, Margot. Probably the girl would have been more scared of you than you of her."

Margot laughed. Stoner was unconsciously amusing.

"You certainly have it all doped out what I should have done, Mr. Stoner, under any and all circumstances. But what I did is done, and I can't see why all this fuss about it now."

"You can't, eh!" He grew threatening. His anger was evidently not far beneath the surface. "Well, you say that to Miss Delamar. She's wild. She's all primed to give you a good calling down."

Margot studied him with a deliberately judicious stare.

"Are you *quite* sure, Mr. Stoner, that Miss Delamar is as wild as all that?"

"Am I quite sure! Say, how do you get that way?" He seemed to become slangy in proportion as he grew angry or amorously familiar. "Go on in and see her, and find out for yourself just how wild she is. She's likely to tell you you're fired."

She felt that he had over-reached himself, and she took quick advantage.

"Oh, really! I thought that no one but you had the power to engage or discharge members of this cast. But if it's in Miss Delamar's province to do what you hint that she may do, why I'll save her and myself the boredom of an interview. I can tender my resignation right here and now."

"Oh, come on!" He hadn't expected her to call his bluff, and she almost grinned into his blustering countenance. "Don't take a fellow up so sharp. Don't be so literal. What I was going to say is this: No matter how mad she is or what she says, I can calm her down afterwards. But you'll have to meet me half way. I'm not going to let myself in for a scrap with Corinne Delamar, unless you promise me two things."

Sheer curiosity to see to what lengths Stoner could conceivably go, made Margot say with a faint smile:

"*Two* things! What are they, Mr. Stoner?"

"First, cut loose from this haunted house bunk. It's going to do you and all of us harm if you persist in being connected with it. I'd like to have you forget the thing ever happened." His words were spoken calmly enough, but she noted a slight twitching of his face.

Certainly the man was nervous. Probably he drank and smoked too much. Most persons did.

"I might possibly be persuaded to buy the security of my job in your picture at that price, although I'd lose a lot of fun." Her levity brought no smile to his lips. Then she said: "And what is the other condition?"

"Well, I suppose you'll think I've got my nerve but I want you to let me be your friend, and see you often. I'm not asking to make love to you—though God knows I'm crazy about you, Margot—but at least give me the chance to help you as I can't while you're running around with Valery."

This last offer of selfish patronage of her career was more bald than previous offers or hints had been, but why let it anger her, she wisely concluded, giving a non-committal smile.

"You're very kind, Mr. Stoner. I'll give the matter thought when I have more time, and not so many absorbing things to think about. Then I'll let you know what I decide to do."

Her delicate irony did not altogether miss its mark. He scowled heavily, but apparently could think of no effective retort, so he stood with shoulders thrown back, and head in air, as she walked off and left him.

A negro maid edged out of the narrow compartment as Margot entered Corinne's dressing room. The star was sitting in a wicker chair beside a table strewn with cosmetics. A disproportionately large mirror hung above the table, flanked by hooks on which were draped a variety of startlingly gaudy Spanish bolero-jackets and shawls. There seemed to be no place for a visitor to sit, so Margot stood, in graceful and well-bred disregard of having to stand.

Corinne was certainly beautiful, Margot thought, looking down at her. Margot was always generous in her enthusiasm over another woman's beauty or charm. The star might be somewhat over thirty, but her strange gold-colored eyes, her ivory-palid cheeks and throat, and her fierce red pouting lips, had all the splendor of early youth.

For an appreciable moment, Corinne did not even turn her head. Then she twisted slowly around in her chair, and looked up at Margot out of narrowed eyes. Her voice was modulated to the velvet softness of the woman whose pose is to appear better bred than she is.

"Miss Anstruther," she began softly, "I understand that this wild story about you in the papers is the result of a play for publicity. Doesn't it strike you as taking an unpardonable liberty, while you have a part supporting me?" At least she had gone directly to the point.

"Who has given you to understand such a thing, Miss Delamar? It's Mr. Stoner, isn't it?"

"Yes. What of it?" Corinne's voice was a trifle less suave.

Of a sudden, and most unexpectedly, Margot wanted intensely to convince Corinne, even to propitiate her, not at all for professional reasons, but because of some deep and mysterious urge to make a friend of the young woman, whose antagonism she had so unwittingly aroused. A swift decision came to her. She would tell the star her so-called ghost story, from beginning to end, or rather to the point it had reached. She would offer neither explanations nor excuses, she would stick to narrative and description of the persons in her little drama.

"Miss Delamar," she began gently, "will you be kind enough to let me tell you frankly just what has happened? I'm sorry if I've done anything to annoy you, but I'd really like you to know the facts at first hand."

Corinne stared at her intently, then she said, pulling out a stool from under the table:

"Please sit down. I'm sorry I haven't a comfortable chair. I'll be glad to hear what you have to say, Miss Anstruther."

Margot's shrewd and watchful eyes did not miss the brightening of Corinne's eyes, or the eager play of her lips, as she listened to the odd and arresting tale. She had held the star's interest and she had won her trust, at least, so far as her mysterious adventure was concerned.

"You certainly put the whole thing in a different light, Miss Anstruther. I'll talk to you again later in the week. I want to think over the matter."

Margot could not restrain the impulse that made her bend over, with an eager smile, as she stood up to go, and say:

"Please do your own thinking, unassisted by Mr. Stoner. For some reason he's determined to put me in the wrong in this matter and make me drop the investigation. I don't know what it's all about, but I can't see why he's so keen about it."

At her first words, Corinne's eyes flashed angrily, but it became clear to her that Margot meant no personal offense, and she nodded a good-by with the first amiable smile that she had ever conferred upon Margot.

On the trip back to town, Margot felt suddenly tired and depressed. Such a fuss and bother and so much confusion to face in the immediate future. She hated rows. She hated having people dislike her or suspect her of mean motives. A sudden overwhelming yearning rushed over her, for the mother who had died when she was sixteen. She had loved her mother, and she had needed her always, but the years in their swift passing, had made her more self-reliant and less given to lonely meditation.

With a return to her normal cheerfulness, Margot put her key in the lock of the front door, and ran up to her room. Gene, the dear boy, was coming to take her to dinner. Her glance fell on a yellow telegram on the table. She ran to it, tore it open and read:

Terribly sorry. Can't come for dinner. Stoner requires that I work

*in the studio tonight. Been transferred to another unit. See you
to-morrow night without fail.*

GENE.

Now, what in creation did that mean! It was most unusual
to transfer a camera man to another unit, in the middle of a
picture. Of course it was done occasionally, but rarely. Besides,
why did Stoner call upon Gene at such short notice! He seemed
to be under her feet at every turn.

She had dinner alone, then returned to her room, after a
brief but not to be avoided conversation with Mrs. Bellew, on
the subject of reporters and other kindred matters. Margot had
some mending to do, and it struck her with ironic force, that, in
the midst of so much mental confusion, she should be sitting
alone in the so-called "haunted" house, mending her stockings.

About a half hour later a tap sounded on her door. Wondering
if it could be Gene, after all, or another message from him, she
opened her door. On the threshold stood Stoner, the landlady
vaguely and apologetically in the dim background of the hall.

CHAPTER IX

HIDDEN MOTIVES

Frederick Stoner stood on the doorsill, holding hat and stick, and striving to smile as if his presence on the threshold of Margot's room was the most natural of all natural happenings.

In Margot's gray eyes, surprise changed swiftly to a cold dismissal. Her aloofness and her obvious disinclination to make the most perfunctory gesture of welcome, brought the landlady forward from where she stood in the shadows of the hall. She put a nervous, apologetic hand on Margot's arm.

"The gentleman said that he was a friend of yours, and your boss, out where you do your play acting. And he said he must see you most particular to-night. And I saw him when he come to your party, so I thought it was all right and I brought him up stairs, my dear."

"It's all right, Mrs. Bellew. Wait a minute, please," she added hastily seeing the landlady's gentle movement toward the head of the stairs. Margot turned steely eyes on Stoner. "What is it you wish to see me about, Mr. Stoner?"

He fumbled his hat and he fumbled his reply.

"Why—er—it's about—in relation to—this matter of the—the mystery you're trying to solve, Margot."

"What do you mean? Another warning such as you gave me this morning?" Her gaze did not waver nor grow less coldly repellent. It was one thing to use diplomacy with Stoner on his own ground, the studio, but when he had the impudence to force himself upon her privacy, without permission or even warning, no diplomacy was required.

"Not that at all," he said hastily. "Nothing of that sort, Miss Anstruther. I've taken the liberty of calling on you to tell you of something that's occurred to me that may be helpful to you."

She frowned, a little puzzled by his manner and his remark. Odd of Stoner, the aggressive, self-sufficient Stoner, to conduct himself in so Uriah Heepish a manner. No unbending came to her reception of him. She stood guard over her threshold with senses alert and watchful.

"I don't think I quite understand. Helpful in what way? Just what do you mean, may I ask?"

He drew himself up and took a firmer grip of his position. Margot read in the pursing of his thick lips, his realization that his deference to her wasn't getting him anywhere.

"After seeing you to-day, Margot, I had a brainstorm, I guess you'd call it. Or call it a hunch, or anything you like. Anyway, something came into my head, and I couldn't wait to tell you all about it. I've got an idea it may go far to clear up your mystery."

Mrs. Bellew's shuddering gasp and quick approach to Margot made her smile. She decided to ask Stoner to come into the room, but the landlady must come also.

"Very well, if you've something interesting to tell me, Mr. Stoner, I'm willing to listen to it. Won't you come in? You also Mrs. Bellew." She stood aside to let them enter, but Stoner drew back.

"Sorry," he said quickly, "but what I have to say is strictly confidential."

Perhaps it was the terseness of his refusal to talk before Mrs. Bellew that decided Margot to interview him unchaperoned. If he had expostulated with excuses or supplications, she would have let him go. He seemed in earnest, and determined, and her quickly aroused curiosity where he was concerned, decided her to dismiss Mrs. Bellew. She turned to the eager dame with a kindly smile.

"I'm sorry, Mrs. Bellew, but if Mr. Stoner feels that he can't discuss the matter except with me, I'm afraid I'll have to ask you to let me withdraw my invitation."

With the door closed on the landlady's retreating figure, Margot wished for a second that she had refused to receive Stoner alone. However, what did it matter! What could he do to her anyway! She indicated a place for the bestowal of his hat and coat, then sat down, pointing to a chair a few feet from her. The preliminary rites of asking permission to smoke, and lighting his and her cigarette, left them at last with the blue haze of smoke and an awkward silence between them. Then Margot asked him what it was he had thought might be of significance in the clearing up of her mystery.

"Well, Margot, by the time I've told you what I've doped out, I hope I'll be able to share honors with you and Mr. Sherlock Holmes. I didn't know I had it in me, but from what I've heard of the details of your story, I believe I've hit on something that you haven't even thought of."

"What *is* it?" She was growing impatient.

"Just a minute now. I don't want to make a fool of myself. I've got a theory and I believe it's workable, but I'm not going to spill it without having some chance to verify it for my own benefit. Of course I've read the stuff in the papers, but I want to see the room for myself, and make certain observations before telling you what I think."

Margot's reasoning powers and sense of justice told her that either she must dismiss Stoner and his theories forthwith, or, if curious to learn what his theory was, and willing to believe in his sincerity in the matter, then she must let him do what he suggested doing, for obviously one couldn't be sure of a theory holding water if it was built on hearsay and second-hand descriptions. It would do no harm to show him the room, in any case. The policeman on guard wouldn't care whom she brought. So she told Stoner that she would show him the room, but that he would have to make his inspection in the presence of the policeman.

They went to the floor below, knocked and were admitted by one of the men who alternated with Quinlan and Boyle. The room was dimly lighted. Evidently it had been decided not to keep guard in the darkness, at least during what the Irishman called the "shank of the evening."

Margot watched Stoner throw a swift, appraising look over the room. He turned to her saying:

"You've left all your own things down here, haven't you?"

"Everything but my personal effects. It seemed best that way."

Stoner addressed the cop with genial familiarity.

"Mind if I give this place the once over? Here, have one?" He gave the cop a fat cigar. "I'll have a squint behind the bed first off the bat, I guess."

Margot couldn't repress a smile of vast amusement, seeing the heavy bulk that was Stoner, get down on all fours and look under the bed. He got to his feet and pulled out the brass bed. Then again he got down on the floor, looked at the walls and along the baseboard. He had the air of doing all this as a matter of form, because all the rest had done the same thing. He turned to Margot with a wave of his arm at the bed, then said, as he pushed the bed back in place:

"Just eliminating. Have to look at every detail of course, the way the rest of the Sherlocks have been doing. Now for something more to the point."

He walked to the door leading to the roof-garden, then walked back to the bed, slowly pacing off the distance. Then he returned to the door, opened it and went out on the roof. Margot could see him gazing at the houses across the way, whose rear windows could be seen with curtains drawn back and bright lights shining. He re-entered the room and went to the window, looked out, then squatted down as he was accustomed to do when looking from certain angles at scenes he was about to have shot. He peered through his hands at the bed and at the floor beside the bed, and again he looked out of the window.

By that time the policeman was gaping in sheer astonishment at the antics of this strange man. Margot, not in the least impressed but wondering what Stoner was getting at, waited in silence. Then he walked to the bed and stood looking down at the rug.

"Show me exactly where you saw that light—where you saw the hand tap the light out."

Margot showed him.

"Do you sleep with your shade up?"

"Yes, usually, so it won't flap with the window open."

"When you leaned over the side of the bed to look for the match you dropped, did you reach your arm over the side a ways before you saw the hand?"

Wondering what he had in his mind, but convinced now that he had something more than an idle curiosity, or a ruse to visit her against her will, Margot told him that so far as she remembered, she did stretch out her arm over the side of the bed before she saw the hand.

"Humph! I thought as much." He grinned with satisfaction, and gave the policeman another cigar. "Now, Margot, I've got every reason for feeling sure of my little theory. Come over here a minute." He walked to the window, opened it, and pointed across the way.

"See that house over there, directly in line with this window?"

"Yes," said Margot, vaguely, standing behind him.

He turned, looking back at the bed.

"See that place on the rug where you saw the light? Right in a line with this window, isn't it?"

Margot nodded, seeing that his comment was correct. A dim suspicion of what he had in mind, had come to her, and with it a slight quickening of interest in what more he had to say.

"Well, go on. What's the answer?"

"My dear young lady, not here. In your present abode, if you don't mind."

Simple and natural of course. No reason why he should air his theory, good or bad, before the policeman. Again Margot's reason made it impossible for her to refuse his request. As the door closed on them, and he sat once more in her easy chair, he smiled, a long, slow smile of utter contentment.

"Don't keep me in suspense," she said with a little laugh.

"Now listen carefully. Anyone standing at the window of that floor in that house I pointed out to you, could flash a light straight into your room. With the clever use of a burning-glass, a spot from a calcium light backed by a reflector could be made to move about and do queer stunts on that rug where the policeman saw the light. You were half asleep you said, and it all happened in a jiffy. I've seen queer things done with a mirror."

She listened, amazed at the ingenuity of his theory.

"But the arm and hand. Calcium light and a burning-glass can do a good deal, but they can't manufacture hands and arms."

"Why, my dear girl, I'm surprised at you. You're too smart to ask such a question! You put your arm over the side of the bed, to reach for the match. Well, it's so simple it's funny! The light and the mirror threw the reflection of your own arm and hand on the rug."

"But," Margot gasped, half convinced. "I *saw* a hand *tap* the match."

"Sure you did. You saw your own hand tap that match. Don't you understand? You saw an apparently ghostly arm and hand on the floor. You were scared stiff, and you didn't know after that *what* you did or didn't do. Automatically you did the very thing you'd started out to do—put out the match. Of course you thought you saw another hand do it. Isn't it clear?"

Margot almost thought it was, but she wasn't quite sure.

"How about the hand and arm seen by Boyle?"

"Good Lord! That doesn't need much explaining, seems to me. Case of superstitious fear. You'd told how *you* saw the hand, so when the calcium light flashed again—pleasant little practical joke, by the way—it stands to reason, doesn't it, that Boyle imagined the same thing you saw, even to tapping out the light."

The logic of the argument was evident, and the theory as to the calcium light and the mirror fairly reasonable. Margot felt sure of that. But deep down in her consciousness was a strange conviction, and it grew as she listened to Stoner and watched his face. It was the conviction that his theory was actually false, that Stoner knew it was false, and that for some reason too obscure to imagine, he was intent upon convincing her of its validity. The queer sensation of distrust of the man was stronger than ever before.

She knew what she must do. She must not let him guess

her distrust of him—foundless as it actually was—nor let him realize that every instinct she possessed was ranged against the sincerity or plausibility of his amazing theory. So she smiled sweetly and said:

"You're tremendously clever, Mr. Stoner. I'd never have thought of such a thing in a thousand years. I shall certainly follow up your theory. It will be easy to find out who lives in that house and in that apartment, and look into the matter of the calcium light."

"Good Lord, you wouldn't be so foolish. You don't suppose anyone given to practical jokes like that is going to admit it. You'd never find out or prove a thing. My only idea in telling you about it is to help you eliminate other theories that may lead you into all sorts of trouble and waste of time."

"I see," she said softly, watching his face through the smoke from her parted lips, her eyes half closed. "And of course, even if we did succeed in proving that the lights were a practical joke, and even if I were convinced that I saw my own hand put out the match, in a moment of hysteria, that wouldn't any of it explain the entrance into my room by way of the roof, of Miss Stella Ball, would it, Mr. Stoner?"

His thick lips pouted. His eyes glowered at her.

"You don't think much of my theory, after all, do you?"

"Yes," she said quickly. "I think it's a marvelous theory, and I think it ought to be given due consideration. But I think that there are other things to consider also."

"What, for instance?"

"Well," she said slowly, "I've still got a little theory of my own about Stella Ball being in some way connected with what I saw."

"Ridiculous!" His exclamation was almost savage in its disgust. "What in the name of God *could* she have to do with it—a common midnight marauder—a little sneak thief!"

"Well, that's all got to be proved, Mr. Stoner."

"Do you mean to say," he stared at her, "that you persist in going on with this silly investigation?"

Quickly she decided to lie to him.

"Well, perhaps you're right. Perhaps it would be a waste of time, and do me harm. Perhaps I'd better take your advice, Mr. Stoner."

She hadn't imagined what her sudden meekness would bring forth. He sprang to his feet, went toward her with outstretched arms and bent over her murmuring:

"You're a darling. You do care a little for me, don't you?"

Margot got to her feet without confusion or haste. She stepped out of his reach and said quietly:

"Mr. Stoner, you must really understand that I don't permit any man to come to my room alone to make love to me. I let you in because you had something important to tell me. Now please leave this love business out of it altogether."

For a moment he stood still looking at her. Then he said:

"Look here, Margot! Is this stuff about being alone in your room, the truth, or are you stalling because you won't let me make love to you here or anywhere else?"

She hesitated; "Let's talk about that some other time," she said gently.

"No! You'll tell me here and now. Valery comes to your room, doesn't he! I'm crazy about you, girl. I can't stand it, I tell you."

There was no mistaking the look in his eyes. No matter what he had come for, nor what his motives might be for elaborating the theory about the lights, she had now to deal with a man whose passions were something to be reckoned with. She moved a step farther away from him. It was an unwise move. Suddenly, and without warning, he sprang across the space between them, seized her, and crushed her in his big arms. She struggled, but he was stronger than she, and he pinned her arms to her sides, and kissed her with furious, pent-up desire; kissed her mouth, her throat, her shoulder, all the time drawing her over to the couch against the wall.

Margot would not scream. It would be a senseless thing to do. With all her rage and strength she fought him. She tore one hand free and with all her force struck him across the mouth. The pain of the blow was nothing, but the fact that she would strike him seemed to change the current of his passion. He let her go and stood looking at her, wiping the blood from his cut lips with his handkerchief.

"Some men," he said slowly, "like to be hit and even bitten by a woman when she's angry. I don't, not when it's clear that the woman hasn't any use for me. I'm through trying to make love to you, Miss Margot Anstruther. And I'm through with a few other things too."

"You had no right to force your kisses on me," she said quietly.

"Let that pass. I'll give you one more chance. Will you or will you not, try to like me and promise to marry me later on?"

"Good Heavens, no!" she said, with so much sincerity that it was like a dash of cold water in his face. He stared angrily, then he said:

"Just one thing more. Will you or will you not, drop this damn foolishness about this mystery stuff?"

"I will not drop it," she said with quiet defiance.

He walked to where he had thrown his hat and coat, and picked them up. Then he stood glowering at her across the room.

"That's all, then. Consider yourself fired from the Superfilm Company. And Valery will find a notice for himself to-morrow morning. I'm damn sorry I gave you the job that day, instead of Lulu."

"You had your good reasons for that, Mr. Stoner." Before he could speak, she added quickly: "Why punish Gene for what I've done?"

"Because I can get at you through him. Also because I'm sick of the very sight of him. But any time you change your mind about marrying me, just let me know. You'll get your job back if you do."

With that he stalked out of the room.

For a long time after Margot put out her light, she lay in the darkness thinking. Strange and ingenious that theory of Stoner's, but far stranger still the motive under the theory. She knew now, she felt it deeply, that he had some motive, other than his desire to force her to drop the case. At least—her thoughts grew a little confused as she grew less wakeful—it wasn't like that exactly. His motive for advancing the theory was obviously to make her drop *her* theories, and the motive back of that was what she couldn't fathom. Well—if for a moment she had been intrigued by Stoner's theory, even to the point of taking it seriously, she had swung back to a rational contemplation of him and his theories. As to her own, they were something to take up with Gene the next day. Poor Gene! It was a shame. But he'd get a job with some other company, and so would she. But not till she'd solved the mystery of the arm that tapped the lighted match—the arm that most positively was *not* her own.

As on the night before, her last waking memory was of those strange, pale eyes of Stoner's, looking at her through a mist of hidden thought and motive and desire.

CHAPTER X

A WITNESS FROM THE DEAD

A long night because of long, long thoughts, then a few hours of sleep and then waking, to see the sun shining through her window. Margot wondered, as she examined her face in the two foot mirror, just how many more sleepless nights she could stand without showing the effects of it. Well, at least she didn't have to rush over to the studio and be irritated by Stoner. It was a shame of course, that she was the cause of Gene being fired, for Stoner would undoubtedly put as many spokes in Gene's wheel as possible. But he already had the reputation of being a clever camera man, and he'd make another good connection in spite of Stoner.

As to herself, Margot worried not at all. She was sorry to leave the charming "Conchita" to the mercy of some substitute who might not understand her passionate Latin temperament as well as she—Margot—understood it, but, oh, what did it all matter! The reflection of herself as a passionate Spanish girl made Margot grin in delighted mockery of her own conception. Of course—she had no doubt about it—she was quite capable of feeling intensely when the right man and the right hour should come along, but Spanish girls didn't have to have the scene so carefully laid. Was it that American women were really cold, or that Spanish women were less fastidious? As to dear old Gene, was he the right one, and was she waiting only for the hour to strike?

She had reached that point in her reflections, over her coffee and rolls, in her room, when she was called to the telephone.

As she heard Gene's voice over the wire, she wondered if it were a case of thought transference. That very moment as he was calling her, she was thinking intently about him.

"Hello, that you, Margot? Say, there's the devil to pay out here. I'm calling from Astoria. I've been given the sack and not a reason offered. And the report out here is that you've had the same dirty deal. Is it true?"

She told him it was, and asked him to come to her house as soon as possible; that she had much to tell him, and something for him to do. His voice sounded more cheerful when he told her that he'd be right over as quick as he could make train connections.

When Gene arrived she gave him both hands and reached her face up for his kiss. He gave it eagerly enough, his eyes glowing with joy at the sight and touch of her. He tried to take her in his arms, but she held him back and smiled an entreaty that he be patient with her.

"We've such a lot to talk about, dear, and so much to do. I promise, Gene, that just as soon as we clear up the mystery of that old room of mine, I'll take your love-making seriously, or else—" She hesitated, striving to be fair and honest with him.

"Or else you'll cut out the love-making altogether, is that it, Margot?"

"Yes, old dear, that's what I meant, but don't get humped about it. Plenty of other bridges to cross first. Who knows, I may discover that I'm desperately in love with you, when I get all the debris out of my mind collected there in the last few days."

Her mood was lightening. Gene always cheered her up. Good sign, she thought, but she refrained from calling his attention to it. Then she told him of Stoner's unexpected call the previous evening. Before she could expatiate on his avowed reason for coming, Gene exploded.

"So *that* was his game, keeping me at work in the studio, and changing me to another unit! I thought it was queer, but I was too dense to connect it with you, Margot."

"No denser than I was. It never occurred to me till after he'd gone. As a matter of fact, he kept my brain too busy with his remarkable theories, until just before he left, and *then* he kept *me* too busy."

Gene stared at her, uncomprehending. She laughed at his expression, then she frowned, remembering with an access of disgust, Stoner's physical attempt to force her hand.

"See here, Gene, if he hadn't fired you I'd not dream of telling you just what happened last night. But as you're no longer under his heel it doesn't matter *what* you know. I'll tell you about my personal encounter with him first. That'll clear the deck for the rest of it, which is really the only interesting thing about last evening."

She described Stoner's attack upon her, his love-making, and his cold fury when she struck him across the mouth. Gene listened with burning eyes and twitching lips, striding up and down the room as Margot talkea.

"So that's that, and a jolly good riddance so far as I'm concerned. I was getting awfully fed-up with his overbearing ways. Until recently I didn't dislike Stoner. Of course I could never have been fond of him, but I liked him—rather—until he antagonized me by his attitude regarding what occurred, and publicity, and all that. He's interesting in a queer, mysterious way. He's got me guessing as to his real motives for working up his elaborate theory and coming here with it. There's *something* I can't reach with my mind, although my imagination plays with it continually."

She described to Gene the visit to the "haunted" room, and Stoner's antics, which filled the policeman with wondering awe, and made Margot want to laugh, up to the moment when he explained his theory.

"And the funny thing about it is that on the surface it sounds reasonable, and it makes you wonder why you hadn't thought of it yourself."

"I suppose," said Gene thoughtfully, "that such a light *could* be sent into a dark room, through an uncurtained window. But it seems to me that unless you'd lost your wits completely, you'd have known the difference between a small circular dancing light, and the tiny upward flare of a lighted match."

"Of course I would," she agreed eagerly. "And as to my hand and arm, really, you know, I'd have to have been utterly mad not to have known the difference between the shadow of an arm and hand, and the real thing crawling over the rug."

"As a matter of fact, it's all bunk, that idea of a calcium light and a burning glass being manipulated so as to throw the shadow of your arm on to the floor." Gene's literal type of mind was more inclined to eliminate the impossible than to consider the possible.

"All the same, there are moments when I wonder a little if it's not stupid of me to take such a negative attitude. After all, Gene, mighty strange things happen, and they're only strange to those who can't understand. I don't know—I'm not dead sure—that a light couldn't be thrown just as he described, and work the same odd tricks. If I were as sure of Stoner himself as I am of my limited knowledge along such lines, I'd be inclined to accept his theory, at least to prove or disprove it, with an open mind."

"You mean that you think he had a hidden motive for propounding his theory?"

"Yes, and besides, he admitted to having given me his theory, expecting that it would clear up the mystery and cause me to drop further investigation, or words to that effect. Now, what puzzles me is whether he wants me to drop the whole thing because of the publicity, or whether. he's using that reason as a screen to his real one."

"Good Lord! You make him out a man of mystery with a subtle brain. That's far-fetched, dear girl. He's the most obvious person I know. He probably concocted that ingenious theory with the hope of convincing you and making you drop the whole thing, but I'll bet a good deal that he's incapable of anything more intricate or sinister than that."

"May—be!" Margot puckered her forehead, and her eyes had a far-seeing expression in their gray depths.

"Well, let's drop that man for five minutes, him and his theories." Gene sat down with an impatient sigh, and lighted a cigarette with nervous fingers. "I think it's about time you gave me the benefit of your own theories, Margot. I'd be grateful to you if you'd give me something to think about besides Stoner and his damn nerve coming here and trying to make love to you. Nice picture before me of his kissing you against your will!"

Margot's sudden laugh brought an angry light to Gene's somber eyes. She leaned toward him and put her hand over his with a little pressure of her fingers, and a smile that strove to express contrition, and failed.

"Silly old thing! Where's your logic, even if you've mislaid your sense of humor. If he'd kissed me *not* against my will, then you *would* have something to groan over. And it's darn lucky for you, little one, that you make it *very* clear that you believe it *was* against my will, for if you didn't, you know what would happen, don't you, Gene?"

"I believe you," he said sullenly, "but if Stoner and I had to meet very often, with you between, something would break sooner or later."

"Well, don't worry. I'm through with Stoner, and so are you. Now, as to my theories. I've got something first I want you to do for me. If you can spare the time I want you to go personally to police headquarters, and make arrangements for Hart and his crowd to meet here at five o'clock. Hart hasn't been here himself for some time. He scorns the case. But you argue that brilliant sleuth into coming. Flatter, cajole him. Tell him I want to call his attention to important new evidence. Make positively sure that he'll be here himself!"

"You've actually got something up your sleeve?"

"If my powers of deduction haven't failed me—yes."

"All right. I'll have Hart here if I have to blackjack him and hire a wheelbarrow. And right now, I'm off to look for another job." He rose and went toward her, holding out his hands.

"Oh, Gene, listen." She was on her feet beside him. "Have you enough to rub along on for a short time?"

"Sure I have, but I don't want to give Stoner the satisfaction of thinking I can't land another job as good as or better than the one he dished me out of, hot off the reel."

"Oh, bother Stoner or what he thinks. In the first place, Gene, I may need every bit of your time in the next few days, and secondly I've got a sort of feeling that you'd better hold off about another job. It's just one of my queer hunches, but if you don't mind very much, and if you can rub along for a while, I do wish you would—dear."

When she said "dear" with precisely that intonation, he would have agreed to commit murder, and he told her so.

Margot spent the intervening hours writing letters and getting mental relaxation in a moving picture house. Nothing, she had found, was quite to be compared with the average movie for complete lulling of all the senses, not to mention the brain.

At a quarter to five Gene came to her room and told her with boyish glee that he had corralled Hart and the others, and brought them to the house in a taxi. They had even stopped at the station house of the district to pick up Quinlan and Boyle. They were all downstairs in her old room, waiting for her.

Eager and impulsive, Margot flew to Gene, threw her arms around his neck and gave him a little hug and a quick kiss on his mouth. No use to hold her, and prolong the kiss. Like a firefly she was off and away, running down the stairs while Gene caught his breath and darted after her.

Hart stood by the mantelpiece, a sarcastic grin and a stiff bow, his greeting to Margot.

"Understand you've got something for us that we weren't bright enough to find for ourselves, Miss Anstruther."

"I believe I have, Mr. Hart." Her smile was as sweet as her low voice. "But I'm wondering if you'll take orders or even suggestions from a mere woman." Her sarcasm was on a par with his, so could not fail to reach him.

"You mean you're going to ask us to do certain things?"

"Well—yes," she said meditatively, "I rather think I am, if you don't mind."

"Anything in reason."

"There are places I want you to examine."

"Places we haven't already searched?"

"Yes. You'll have to get a crowbar."

"We shouldn't wreck this woman's house, Miss Anstruther."

"It won't be necessary," she said quietly.

Hart's scorn became more obvious, but he sent one of his men to borrow the implement at a nearby hardware shop. Then Margot, who had remained silent while the man was out getting the crowbar, pointed to the brass bed.

"Please move that aside and turn back the rug. I don't think you'll be disappointed, Mr. Hart."

"Trapdoor, eh," Hart muttered. "That your idea?"

"Go ahead and look," she said quickly.

Hart made no move toward the bed. He stood looking at Margot with shrewd, quizzical eyes. Then he said:

"You had a man up here last night, I understand, taking measurements and giving the place an inspection."

"Yes." Margot's monosyllable was spoken with a friendly inflection.

"Private detective?"

"Oh, dear no!" She could not suppress a smile at thought of Stoner in the role of private detective.

"What's the joke?" Hart neither looked nor spoke as if he considered it one.

"No joke at all, Mr. Hart." She became suddenly very grave. "Merely a casual visitor who had heard what happened to me and wanted to look over the ground himself. Just curiosity."

"My man who was here last night, said that your friend did certain things and made comments that sounded as if he had some theory about your ghost. Was it your friend who suggested the trapdoor?"

"No. He did have a theory, but it followed very different lines."

"Well, give us his theory. I'd like to hear it," Hart spoke a little brusquely.

"It's an entirely personal matter, Mr. Hart, and in my opinion doesn't bear on this case at all. At any rate, I'm conceited enough to prefer my own theory. If nothing comes of it, then we can look into the one advanced by my caller last night."

Hart gave her a long, speculative look, then, without another word, he told two of his men to push back the brass bed.

The men pulled out the rug which covered the drab old carpet that extended to the wall on both sides. Then they ripped at the carpet where it was tacked down around the edges. In a few minutes they had bared the planking. A thick layer of dust covered the floor, yet even through the dust, dark stains were visible. Clearly defined as well, was a square outline some two feet each way, near the wall where the head of the bed had been.

Hart turned abruptly to Margot.

"Have you known about this all along?"

"No, I haven't. I merely reached the conclusion that some such thing must be there." Her steady look at him seemed to say that such a conclusion was too simple and obvious to have evaded any mind trained to such analysis.

Hart went down on his knees and began to prod with his fingertips.

"Seems to be stuffed with some kind of wadding. Looks as if it hadn't been touched for months." Hart spoke without looking up. He was intent on the discovery they had made.

"Suppose you open it," Margot suggested quietly.

An atmosphere of mystery amounting to horror pervaded the room. Gene stared from Hart on his knees, to Margot standing erect and watchful. Quinlan and Boyle frowned fiercely and strove to preserve a stoicism which made Margot want to laugh, even though she trembled with excitement. Eager to a point where it was difficult to restrain her mad desire to find what lay under all that dust and wadding or whatever it was, nevertheless she felt a cold, shuddering dread of what they might discover.

Hart rose to his feet and asked for the crowbar. With the help of one of his men he drove it down into a crack. They heaved and wrenched, then with so little final effort that it seemed as if mystery and horror laughed and mocked their struggles with the crowbar, a trapdoor lifted and fell over on the floor; an indubitable trapdoor it was.

For once, Hart lost his superior air of composure. He spoke quickly, with excited gasps.

"There's a big compartment here. Looks as if it's hollowed from the central stone support of the house."

Margot was on her knees beside him, and Gene was standing over her.

"Look and see what's in it," she commanded.

Hart reached into the hole and drew out a fire ax, such as hangs beside a bucket of water in the hallways of public buildings.

"There's that," he muttered, holding the ax up for inspection.

He reached again into the hole, probed eagerly, then gave a sudden cry of surprise and loathing. He drew his hand out with a desperate jerk and dropped a horrifying object on the floor. Margot suppressed a scream, and Boyle didn't. His cry was almost a wail as if he had seen the Banshee in his own country. Gene bent swiftly and drew Margot to her feet, holding her against him. No one looked at anyone else. There was something else to look at.

On the floor, where Hart had dropped it, was the severed and withered arm of a woman. A desiccated, mummy-like arm. The hand was tightly clenched. On the upper side it was marred from wrist to knuckles by a huge burn resembling a chocolate-colored birthmark.

No one spoke, no one stirred, no one removed his gaze from the object on the floor—a gaze of horror and utter confusion of thought and emotion. Margot shuddered and pressed closer to Gene. Then she whispered to him. The power of reasoning had returned with a flash of insight. The silence of the room was broken by a low, agonized moan.

"God have mercy on us all!" It was Shane Boyle, down on his knees in an attitude of prayerful supplication. "Sure, it's the GHOST of this arm we've been seein."

"The arm it is, I say, of Stella Ball." Strange that it should have been the material-minded, slow-witted Quinlan who spoke.

CHAPTER XI

WHOSE HAND?

For a few seconds no one spoke, either to contradict or agree with Quinlan. And no one stirred or removed his gaze of stunned surprise and fascinated loathing from the severed arm, with its hand clenched and disfigured by so unsightly a scar.

Hart turned a sudden look upon Margot, a look of penetrating suspicion, that made Gene frown angrily, taking a step forward and holding firmly to Margot's arm. Hart's expression was easy to interpret, but it was such an unexpected turning of the tables that, for a second, she could not cope with it.

"May I inquire, Miss Anstruther, if this is a pleasant little practical joke you've staged for our benefit, with the obvious intention of keeping yourself in the limelight, or if it's just the last act in a comedy you began a few nights ago, from the same motive?"

Margot's face flamed with an intensity of anger she had not

supposed herself capable of. Gene gave a low exclamation of indignant disgust, and made a threatening movement nearer to Hart. She drew him back and whispered to him to let her handle Hart. Her breath came short and fast, as she struggled for self-control. It was too outrageous of the detective, but why should she care what he thought or said? The facts, so far as they had gone, would prove themselves, and she felt thrillingly competent to handle the situation from this point to whatever climax might be lurking in mystery. The hot flow of blood receded from her face, leaving her calm and very cool, physically and mentally. She returned Hart's exasperating stare with an expression as mild as it was compelling.

"Mr. Hart," she began quietly, "it will probably be impossible, and certainly it's quite unnecessary, for me to convince you of anything which you've made up your mind not to believe. To be quite frank, I honestly do not think that your opinion of me or of my motives will make any more difference in the conduct of this case, or its ultimate disposal, than your opinion makes a difference to me personally."

Gene squeezed her arm in excited admiration for her spirit and her clever retort. The other men looked down at the floor, or at the ceiling or out of the window; anywhere but at Hart. He grew a little paler, and his mouth twisted with an ugly sneer. Then he seemed to think better of it, or sudden change came to his mood. His level look into her eyes was less antagonistic, and his manner conveyed more respect for the girl who stood so quietly regarding him.

"You still claim that every word you told Quinlan and Boyle that first night, and all you said subsequently to me, was absolutely true?"

"If my word is of any consequence to you, Mr. Hart, yes, I do still claim just that."

"And you knew absolutely nothing about this trapdoor or what I found down in that hole?"

"Absolutely nothing, Mr. Hart." Her quiet statement was more convincing than an oath.

"Well,—I'll be damned!" Hart sounded quite sincere, and more mystified than Margot had ever hoped to have him admit, even tacitly.

"Gene, please go downstairs and ask Mrs. Bellew to come up here right away. And prepare her mind about—that—" she glanced toward what lay on the floor; "so she won't get hysterical up here."

Gene knew from the sudden darkening and widening of her eyes, that her keen brain had swiftly adjusted itself to the facts, had seized upon whatever was concrete, and was intent upon pursuing her deductions without loss of time. As he went quickly to the door, she turned again to Hart.

"Have you any explanation, Mr. Hart?"

Hart shrugged his thin shoulders, and stared down at the gruesome object.

"Not yet," he said laconically. Then he added a little sulkily. "You've sprung a bit of mysterious dirty work on me, and you can't expect me to hand out an explanation till I've followed up the clues."

"Surely you regard this discovery as part of the investigation, don't you? It isn't a *new* case."

"It's the first proof I've had that there's anything you could call a case," he said doggedly.

"Well, at least you'll agree with me that sane persons in a strictly material world, couldn't possibly conduct this case on the basis of its having any element of the supernatural."

Little did Hart suspect that Margot was actually, at that moment, fighting the temptation to let precisely that element creep into her emotions if not into her reflections. To speak so scornfully to Hart of things supernatural, was the best way, she felt, to harden her own mental attitude.

"I've never said or thought that any such foolishness should be taken seriously for a minute." Hart was certainly sanely balanced.

A low murmur from Shane Boyle focussed attention on him. He was crossing himself, his expression between ecstasy and despair. Margot exchanged a smile with Hart, then she said:

"You agree with Quinlan, don't you, Mr. Hart, that that horrible arm down there belonged to the girl Stella Ball?"

"Good God! What next. I'd like to know!"

"It seems clear enough to me," she pursued slowly. "In fact, that dead and mutilated thing is as eloquent as if it were a live thing talking to me."

"So far as I'm concerned, it doesn't mean a thing, except that a woman had her arm cut off."

"How long ago, could you form any idea?"

Hart stooped and scrutinized the grim relic. He studied the interior of the recess in the flooring, as well as he could without putting his head down into it. He stood up finally and spoke with respect for Margot's mystery, for the first time since he had come on the case.

"That arm hasn't decayed. As far as I know anything about it, I'd say it's because it's been in that hole close to the main chimney of the house, which has preserved a very high temperature and kept the hole dry."

Margot followed his deductions with eyes and lips expressing intensity of interest and the first respect for Hart's intelligence which he had so far inspired in her.

"Sounds absolutely logical," she said excitedly. "How long has the arm been in the hole, would you say?"

"Well, judging by the condition of the flesh, I'd say about three months."

"Good!" She was trembling now from head to foot. "My training in medical college leads me to agree with you." She turned at the sound of the door opening, and swept a quick glance over Mrs. Bellew, whose eyes were red, her face quivering with nervous fear. Then Margot, looking from Mrs. Bellew to Hart, and back again to the landlady, said quietly:

"Stella Ball disappeared from this room exactly three months ago, didn't she, Mrs. Bellew?"

"Three months—yes, yes, three months," the poor woman mumbled, almost beyond speech as her horrified gaze fixed itself on the desiccated arm.

"Damn queer coincidence." Hart seemed to find it difficult to accept Margot's deductions.

"Please, Mr. Hart," she said impatiently, "just for the sake of argument, admit that there's more than a coincidence in this. Just follow me closely. Admitting that this arm was once a part of Stella Ball's body, there's something else to explain. Up to the date of the crime—of course there's been a crime! Just look at the way that arm was severed from the body! Well, up to that time, or, to put it differently, up to the time she disappeared, so far as Mrs. Bellew can tell us, neither of her hands was marked in this extraordinary way. Isn't that true, Mrs. Bellew?" Margot put her hand gently on the woman's trembling arm, trying to soothe her.

"No, no, dearie," Mrs. Bellew's voice, weak from shock, dropped to a whisper. "Her hand was just like yours and mine, dearie."

Hart stood contemplating the scarred hand. Then he met Margot's inquiring eyes.

"What do you make out of it, Mr. Hart?" she asked courteously.

"Granting, as you said, for the sake of argument, that the arm and hand down there belong to the girl Stella, then I'd say that she must have been fooling with some sort of acid. Poisoned the hand."

Margot gave Mrs. Bellew's arm an encouraging pat, then she went over and stood looking down at the ugly scar. Suddenly she bent closer. Someone started to speak and she threw out her hand with a quick gesture compelling silence. Gene moved closer to her, then he touched her shoulder and said softly:

"What is it, Margot?"

She stood up slowly, her fine eyes bright with the effort of concentrated thought and sudden inspiration.

"It's not an acid burn. I'm sure of that," she said slowly.

"How can you be sure without a chemical analysis?"

In Hart's limited way he was certainly more intelligent than she had supposed.

"You're right, of course, Mr. Hart, or rather you would be if it wasn't for the fact that in my laboratory work I made a special study for a time, of the effect on skin and flesh of certain acids. Also, I was much interested in the study of radium burns."

She stopped, looking significantly from Hart to the hand on the floor.

"You don't mean—you can't think that's a radium burn, Margot!" It was Gene and not Hart who challenged her obvious deduction; Gene, with wide, astonished eyes staring at her.

"Yes, Gene, that's just what I do mean. That's a radium burn or I know nothing at all about radium, and I ought to know a good deal about it," she asserted calmly.

Hart seemed nonplussed. He looked helplessly from Margot to the floor, and finally he said:

"Most people know something about radium, enough anyway to realize that it does very queer things. But this does seem a little too queer even for radium."

"Why?" Margot questioned him eagerly. "If you admit or accept all the other much queerer things about this weird case, I can't see anything especially remarkable in Stella Ball having burned her hand with radium. If you hold it in your hand long enough, it does burn, you know," she ended with a smile.

"Held it in her hand long enough," he repeated vaguely. "What do you mean? Held it in her hand before her hand was cut off?"

A sound that suggested that someone in the room was choking, brought Hart's head around with a jerk to where his men were standing, at rigid attention. But every face was composed to expressionless immovability, except that if he had looked a little closer, he would have caught the faintest quiver at the corners of Quinlan's broad mouth—Quinlan with his Irish humor up his sleeve. Margot struggled desperately with a laugh, then she said, with a conciliating smile:

"Mr. Hart, you're not Irish, I know, but you'll have to admit you made an Irish bull that time. How in the name of glory could the girl have gotten radium into her hand *after* it was severed?"

Hart managed a smile. Not so bad for Hart, Margot thought, watching him. Then he returned to his subject with a new attack.

"Aren't you running a little wild, Miss Anstruther? Radium! Why, that's stuff for scientists! How could people living in a rooming house get hold of any of it?"

"Such a person might conceivably have stolen it," she said smoothly.

Of a sudden Hart's eyes narrowed and his eyebrows met over his eyes. He stared ahead of him, at nothing apparently, then he met Margot's intense scrutiny.

"I'll tell you what you're thinking, Mr. Hart, for it's what I'm thinking myself. You've just remembered that a while ago, the Fellowe Institute lost some radium, a fraction of a gram in weight, but valued at $75,000. You're remembering also that every other particle in the world is accounted for. I happen to know that the police have been trying for months to find the thief. May I ask if you haven't had orders to watch out for him yourself?"

He stared at her, divided between amazement at what she had said, and wondering, if slowly dawning, admiration for the girl herself.

"You're right, I have been. I suppose there's some connection, but I can't see it." That he should be willing to concede the logic of any deduction of hers struck Margot as amusing.

"This is what I make out of it," she said, looking from Hart to Gene. "Of course I know nothing about the theft from the Fellowe Institute, except what I read in the papers—what I suppose you both read at the time. But I've got this advantage. I've been a medical student. However, it seems to me if you accept my judgment that the burn is from radium, you ought to feel as if the trail were fairly hot."

"Granting that you're right about the burn, then all I've got to say, Miss Anstruther, is that you're a clever young woman."

The detective's low bow gave Margot a pleasant little thrill. At last she had conquered his cynical distrust of her, of her motives, and her theories. It was a gesture of mental as well as physical obeisance.

"I suppose the next thing on the cards," he said, moving toward the door, "is to grill the girl Stella—I mean in connection with the Institute job."

"Wait a minute!" Margot said eagerly. "Have you a clear idea how a radium burn is produced, Mr. Hart?"

"Not exactly."

She told him as simply and briefly as possible that radium

eternally dissipates itself in infinitesimal particles. These pass, she explained, through anything they encounter; steel or stone are no obstacles to this stream of atoms. At long range, they are harmless to human tissues, but if the contact is close, they scorch and kill.

"I get you," he said, obviously trying to grasp something that eluded him.

"Not quite," she said gently. "But you will in a minute, as soon as you pry open those withered fingers." She looked down at the thing on the floor.

Hart stared from her to the hand, and Mrs. Bellew and Boyle gave vent to low groans, and crossed themselves. In silence— a silence that vibrated with tense excitement—Hart bent down and tried to open the tightly clenched hand. It had long been rigid, and Margot saw his shoulders shake with sudden shrinking disgust. Then he bent back the fingers just enough to draw from the palm a small object which he held up to the light. It was a metal container about as large as the capsule in which druggists sell a dose of quinine.

More dazed than elated, he said doubtfully:

"Looks like what the Institute's been trying to find."

"That's exactly what it is," Margot said excitedly, taking it from him and examining it. She handed it back to Hart saying: "Better be careful of it, Mr. Hart!" She smiled at the nervous haste with which he laid it in an empty ash tray. "Oh, it's not that bad. You could hold it for a while without getting burned. What I meant is to be careful because it's so precious. And it's so small it's easy to lose."

"*Now,* what, Miss Anstruther? I'm inclined to take your orders in this case from now on."

"I should say, now go and get Stella Ball and confront her with this evidence. This may shock her into telling us her story."

"I'll have her here right after supper," said Hart.

"Fine! You'll find me here, too."

Margot smiled at Gene, took Mrs. Bellew gently by the arm, and together the three of them left the room of mystery.

CHAPTER XII

STELLA'S STORY

A comforting assurance to the nervous and anxious landlady, a promise to let her be present at the grilling of Stella Ball, later in the evening, and an impulsive little kiss on the poor woman's pale cheek, then Margot led Gene to her room, saying that she had something to tell him.

"Gene, I've got a little plan, and it includes you, old dear. We've got two hours before Hart brings that girl here. Of course we'll have to have a bite to eat. I'm not hungry—too excited—but you must be, and I ought to eat anyway. *Then*—" She paused with dramatic suspense. "Then, my dear, we'll go to see a motion picture!"

If she had suggested a casual trip to the moon, he couldn't have looked at her with more astonishment.

"A motion picture! I thought you hated them, and of all things to-night, when you've got so much on your mind."

"That might be reason enough, seeing that they usually put me to sleep. Just what I need right now, to rest my nerves."

"Oh, all right," he agreed amiably.

"But," she said with a laugh, "that *isn't* the reason I want to go to a picture to-night. I want to go to a very *special* picture. One that was directed by Stoner."

"What's the big idea?" Gene was more mystified than before.

"I'll tell you later. I missed the first showing of this picture, but I've heard that it contains a curious feature. You know how one idea gives birth to another, when your mind's all keyed up? Well, in the last fifteen minutes, while I've been concentrating on what we found down there in that room, my poor, weak brain's been literally flooded with some new and very strange thoughts. Very strange indeed," she repeated dreamily.

"You mean—thoughts connected with Stoner?"

"Oh, yes," she said softly, "very much connected with Stoner. Of course they're only *thoughts*—they're too vague yet to be even speculations, let alone deductions. Just thoughts, but such very intriguing ones, Gene."

"I daresay, when you get ready to, you'll let me have the benefit of your precious thoughts." Gene was just a trifle impatient and she laughed at him.

"Hold your horses, old darling. All in good time, I'll share my thoughts with you, and perhaps other more important things as well." She threw him a provocative smile, but evaded his arms, as he plunged at her, trying to seize her.

"*Perhaps,* I said. In the meantime, as I told you before, my brain's fairly reeking with mystery. Come on! Let's go eat!"

"Just a minute, Margot," he urged. "Tell me about the picture. What picture is it? I mean, what's so curious about it?"

"I can't tell you now. I want you to see it and get your own fresh impression from it, without being influenced by any reflection of mine."

"What the deuce can a picture directed by that boob have

to do with the mystery of Stella Ball, and your room, and the radium! You're a funny kid! Well, come. I'm starved, even if I am madly in love, and almost insane with curiosity."

An Italian dinner with red wine served in teacups, made Margot more irrepressibly tantalizing and irresistibly alluring than usual. The food was negative, but youth and red wine in a teacup leave the spirit aloof from such gross material considerations.

They spent only a half hour in the little restaurant, then walked quickly over to Eighth Avenue, where they found seats in a small theater for *The Masque of Life*. It was a photoplay of pretentious melodrama, verging on the grotesque, which had been completed for the Superfilm Company, some weeks before. It had had a short run—unhonored and unsung—on Broadway, and was now making the round of the smaller houses.

Through the tiresome opening reels, Margot sat, sleepily content, her hand held fast in Gene's. Then, toward the close of the picture, she aroused to sudden interest, and gave Gene's hand a violent squeeze. She whispered something to him, then she sat very still and intent, watching the action develop along strange lines.

An inventor was shown at work upon a devilish contraption with which he planned to destroy New York. Its motive power was to be—*radium*. The single word was flashed in huge letters across the screen. This time it was Gene who tightened his clasp on the fingers he held. The authority of science was acclaimed as the basis for the weird results obtained by the villain. Certainly there was an uncanny thrill in his first experiment with his diabolical machine.

It was shown as functioning at night. A mysterious aura glowed about it. Rays like forked lightning darted from its entrails.

"Good Lord!" Gene's excited whisper was close to Margot's ear. "I see your point!"

"Do you?" she whispered back. "Then work out a theory, but don't tell me till later. I want to get a grip on my own ideas first."

They sat to the end of the picture, and through a Sennett comedy, because, as Margot explained, she wanted to sit quietly where she was, until it was time to return to the house. He told her that he'd probably explode if she didn't let him tell her something that he was as sure of as that he held her hand in his. But she whispered, with a low laugh, that if exploding would relieve his feelings, she'd hate to stand in his way. As far as comparing notes was concerned—nothing doing, she said sternly, until later.

At eight o'clock they returned to Margot's house of mystery. In the hallway they found Cornelius Hart and Quinlan. Between them stood Stella Ball. Her eyes were dull and sullen, her mouth bitter. A handcuff was fastened to her left wrist, while the other end dangled uselessly.

"You said you wished to speak to this girl, Miss Anstruther," said Hart casually. "She's at your service." Margot accepted his veiled remark as a suggestion that she take charge of Stella.

Evidently Hart had been careful to raise no suspicion in Stella's mind that she was to be subjected to a test of any kind. Black-browed and fierce, her glance swept over the faces of the men, then rested on Margot's with defiant scorn. Margot, open-minded at all times, and generous in her estimates, found it quite natural that this young thing—potentially a criminal perhaps, but certainly not a coward in spirit or flesh—should regard a girl of Margot's class with the disdain that those who dare much feel for those who are sheltered from all daring.

Stella had grown thinner and paler in jail. Her stubborn will seemed unbroken. Her thin lips parted as if the impulse moved her to protest against she knew not what. Then her mouth shut stubbornly, and she gave Hart an ugly look. She promised to be a difficult subject, that much was sure. Margot tingled at the prospect of the encounter. It would be even more thrilling than she had anticipated.

"I'm sure," she said gently, "that Stella Ball will be able and willing to help us clear up certain things." Her tone was noncommittal, but her penetrating look into the girl's eyes was kindly. "I'll go up ahead," she said to Hart. "I just want to take a look around."

He understood her intent—to make sure that nothing had been disturbed—and he, together with the girl, Gene and Quinlan, followed slowly up the stairs.

Margot found Boyle and another man standing solemnly on guard in the room where so many fateful things had occurred. How many more were destined to happen there? she wondered vaguely. Mrs. Bellew was already in the room. Margot smiled, understanding that the inquisitive and excited creature was determined not to lose a moment of the new scene soon to be enacted.

Margot took quiet charge of the situation. She cautioned the landlady not to speak unless addressed, and asked her to sit still in one corner of the room, not too far away from the center of the stage—meaning the brass bed and the trapdoor and the gruesome object on the floor. She told the two policemen to stand on either side of the trapdoor. Then she called to Hart to bring in Stella Ball.

The girl had been directed to walk a little ahead of the three men, thus blocking her only way of retreat. It was inevitable that she would see the bed pushed out from the wall, the hole in the floor, and the withered arm lying on the bare planking, on reaching the threshold of the room. Her foot was scarcely on the doorsill when she jerked back on her heels and stared with distended eyes.

No one spoke. If what she saw could not shake her, words would be wasted. The moment of hostile silence was calculated to force confession, but she seemed unconscious of it. All her senses were concentrated upon the thing on the floor and its significance to her. Horror and fear were the emotions most clearly expressed on her hitherto impassive face. Then it hardened, and her lips grew tight. She paid no attention to anyone but Hart. At him she looked accusingly.

"Done me dirt, ain't you?" she said coolly. "Got the goods on me, then brought me here to spring it on me, and watch me jump. Well—whacher goin' to do about it?"

Margot came quickly nearer to the girl.

"We won't do anything about it—I mean we won't do *you* any harm if you'll tell us what you know. Why did you do it?"

"Do what?" she asked sharply, staring at Margot.

"Oh, of course, you don't know that we found the radium in that hand on the floor—*your* hand, Stella. How did you get hold of it?"

"I've been a fence for a long time, that's how," she said sulkily.

Margot exchanged a glance of surprised understanding with Gene and with Hart, then she said gently:

"Tell us how you got mixed up with a crook who stole radium, and how you lost your arm?"

"I lost it all right," she said with an expression of such acute distress that Margot said quickly:

"We're all awfully sorry for you. But you really must help the law in every way. If you don't, I'm afraid it may go hard with you."

"I told ya before, I aint committed a crime. The law can't do nothin' to me."

"See here, my girl!" Hart spoke impatiently. "Maybe you haven't done away with anybody, but being a professional receiver of stolen goods isn't one of the things the law smiles at. Better come across and give us all the dope!"

"We know a good deal about you already," Margot prompted gently. "We know that you lived in this room and we know why." (Margot had jumped to a certain conclusion in the last few seconds.) "That trapdoor leads to a place that's fine as a receptacle for stolen radium, or anything small like that. We know that you took this room for that sole purpose."

"How d'you know?" Stella could not be tripped so easily. "Oh, well," she added disgustedly, "I guess it don't take much savvy to know that much. But I wasn't the first one to do it. The woman who was here before gave me the tip."

Mrs. Bellew gave a low cry, quickly stifled in her handkerchief.

"You had a confederate in this house, didn't you?" Margot held the girl's eyes as she added slowly: "An elderly man by the name of Murchison, who lived on the top floor?"

"By jove, Margot, you're wonderful!" It was unprofessional, but Gene could not restrain his joy at her acumen. It was easy now to follow her deductions step by step.

"I got to know him after I come here," Stella said, staring at the floor. "He worked in some sort of a hospital, he told me."

"You mean, don't you, the Fellowe Institute?" Margot corrected her gently.

"Yeah, guess that was it. He was a pretty slick pickpocket. Used to bring me watches and things to keep. Then one day he said he'd swiped a tube of stuff that was worth more'n fifty thousand dollars. I thought he was lying till I saw the fuss in the papers about the radium."

A gentle question or two from Margot, and the girl told her how she had hidden the radium in the secret chamber, Murchison having promised her a big commission when he should sell the stuff. He had told her that it might take a long time to sell it, because only doctors and professors would want to buy it, and most of them would be leery about stolen goods.

Suddenly Stella's voice trailed off and her face grew very white. She closed her eyes and a long shudder shook her thin shoulders.

"What's the matter?" The sympathy in Margot's voice brought a quick response.

"I was just thinkin'," Stella mumbled, "of the night when things went on the blink."

"You mean—" Margot took her up quickly, "the night you disappeared—three months ago?"

"Yeah." The girl gave her head a sudden upward jerk. Fixing her haggard young eyes on a spot where the light reflected on the footrail of the brass bed, she finished her astounding narrative. Her words came in a quick-running monotone, almost without punctuation. The substance of her story was this:

Her acquaintance with Murchison had developed during several weeks. One day he told her to expect him that night at ten o'clock, with a customer. She had things ready when they arrived. She had turned back the carpet and opened the trap-door with an ax. Murchison brought with him a fat man whom she had never seen. An argument took place between the two men. The fat man, it seemed, had no idea of buying the radium. He wanted only to rent it for a week, and he offered Murchison five hundred dollars. Murchison objected and ended by getting very "sore," as Stella expressed it, He told his customer that the deal was off.

Then Stella took a hand in the fray. She was dead broke at

the time and had counted on the commission promised her by Murchison. She took the part of the strange man, with the result that a real scrap started. Murchison, although elderly, was strong and wiry, and a match for the fat man, whose muscles were soft. But between the two of them—Stella and the stranger—Murchison was kept busy, and Stella managed to grab the little tube of radium out of his hand. At that point of her narrative, she moved her gaze from the bedrail to Margot's intensely interested eyes.

"The old fool went crazy mad when I did that. He was a sort of a nut, anyway. The next I knew, he'd got ahold of the fire ax and chopped at me. I went down on the floor. The blade nicked me at the elbow joint and went clean through. I started to scream, but somebody put his hand over my mouth and I fainted. I came to in a private hospital. Never found out who took me there, but somebody paid the bills and kept me there till I got well. That's all I know for sure."

No one spoke for a brief instant, then Hart said judiciously:

"One or the other of those two crooks must have known something about putting a tourniquet above the elbow, or you'd have bled to death through the artery."

"Of course it must have been one of them who took you to the hospital. Have you any suspicion at all which of them it was—although it doesn't really matter," Margot added quickly.

"I'd take a bet it wasn't the old fellow. He was so sore at me I guess he'd have liked to stick me down that hole along with my arm. Then too, I don't believe he'd have dared go to a place like a hospital. The other guy wasn't a real crook, or I miss my guess."

"Did you realize when Murchison chopped off your arm, that the radium was clasped in that hand?" Margot asked her.

"Well—s'pose I did, if I thought of anythin' but the pain and the bleedin'. But when I got my head clear, in the hospital, I figured they'd be too scared to check up on that. I figured they'd throw the arm and the ax into the hole, and put back the carpet so's to hide the bloodstains."

"And figuring that way, you broke in here by way of the roof, to get the radium?" Hart spoke rapidly, then turned to Margot with a slight inclination of his head. "Excuse me, Miss Anstruther, but my curiosity got the better of me."

"It really doesn't matter who asks the questions, Mr. Hart, or rather who asks them *first*," she added with a smile.

"What did you suppose I'd come for?" Stella threw Hart a glance of amused scorn. "Me health maybe, or maybe me arm? *Sure,* I come for the seventy-five-thousand-dollar goods. Couldn't pass up a little thing like that," she said with a twisted smile. "There was a good chance the old devil'd beaten me to it, but it was worth a try."

Hart asked her if she knew the present whereabouts of Murchison. She said she didn't. Then Margot asked her to describe the customer who had started all the trouble.

"Well," said Stella, doubtfully, "I can't just remember what he looked like, except he was fat—too fat. I hate fat men." Her gamin sense of humor made her throw a quick glance from man to man, and add, with a boyish grin: "Guess I ain't steppin' on anybody's toes in this room."

Margot smiled to note the unconscious preening of Hart, who was the thinnest man of them all. Then she asked Stella if that was positively all she could remember and to tell them of the events leading up to and following the dramatic incident of the fight over the radium.

"I've told you all I know, s'help me God!"

The thin, worn face of the girl, and her tragic eyes, carried conviction as no words could have done. Again there, came a silence which Hart waited for Margot to break, but she only stored with dark, thoughtful eyes, straight before her. Then Hart said respectfully:

"You've done a fine piece of work, Miss Anstruther. The rest of this case should be plain sailing."

"You think so?" she said gently. "How about the lights on the floor and the hand that put them out?"

"That seems clear to me," Hart said confidently. "The radium shone through the floor and the carpet. You explained to us, you remember, that radium rays can pierce through anything. I take it that these rays also revealed an outline of the dead arm—a sort of mirage in the dark, which, naturally, seemed to you and to Boyle, to extinguish the flame."

Margot turned quickly to Gene. "Do you see it that way, Gene?"

"Yes," he said with conviction. "That part of the mystery was cleared up, so far as I was concerned, while we were looking at that queer picture to-night—Stoner's picture. I took for granted that was what you wanted me to deduce from it."

"I'm sorry, Gene, but that *wasn't* what I wanted you to get from that picture. I rather hoped you'd get something else out of it."

"I did," he said eagerly, "or rather I *do*, looking back at it in the light of what's been thrown on the mystery here, to-night."

"Righto! We'll take that up later." She gave him a warning look, then turned to Hart.

"It sounds convincing, the way you put it, Mr. Hart, but I'll have to tell you that radium cannot project a mirage. Its rays are invisible to the naked eye, except with the aid of a special apparatus. The hand and the lights had nothing whatever to do with radium."

"Holy Mother Mary!" Boyle, indifferent to the stares of his audience and callous to their amused grins, crossed himself for the third time. "Then it was a ghost, after all, Miss?"

"That all depends on just what you mean by a 'ghost.'" Margot's smile at Boyle was enigmatic, as she intended it to be, not only to poor Boyle but to every other person in the room.

CHAPTER XIII

WILL-O'-THE-WISP

The love of drama which lay back of Margot's histrionic talent, and which had always made her create situations out of material from which the unimaginative could weave nothing, now made her eyes shine with the sheer delight of the artist who first creates and then interprets. The scientist was in the background for the moment; only the actress stood smiling and looking from one mystified face to another.

Gene's puzzled frown changed suddenly to a smile of encouragement and understanding. He caught her mood and threw it back to her, with a humorous sympathy that quickened a tenderness for him which flashed in her eyes and curled the corners of her mouth. It was rather thrilling to have such an absorbed audience, inclusive of Gene with his adoring belief in her powers of analysis, and cleverness in general.

"If it won't bore any of you," she began, her smile broadening at their eager denials, "I'll tell you just what my process of deduction has been in this case, up to this point. Mr. Hart, what puzzles you most of all?"

"The matter of the lights on the carpet," he said quickly.

"Isn't that funny," she said, her smile solely for Hart. "That's just where I was going to begin my explanation. Well—first of all, the flame *I* saw was my own match, of course. But the one Boyle saw was of a very different character—a most singular character, in fact. Moreover, if there had been witnesses here at favorable moments, both before and after, I believe they would have seen it too."

"Sure, it was just like me own poor luck. I'll be thinking, that it was meself was seein' the quare lights!" Boyle was far too engrossed with his subject to be conscious of Hart's glance of disapproval.

"That *was* a question of luck, you're right." Margot smiled at Boyle. "It was the merest chance that others didn't see the same thing. Have any of you ever heard of what is called in Latin the *ignis fatuus?*"

Gene nodded his head, and Hart said: "You mean what's commonly called the will-o'-the-wisp?"

"Glory be!" It was Boyle again, irrepressible and oblivious of his superior's scowl. "It's what you'll be seein' in graveyards of a dark night!"

"Some call it a 'corpse-candle,'" contributed Quinlan, not to be outshone by his comrade. "There's many in the auld country that's seen it, I'm tellin' you, Miss."

"Surely," agreed Margot. "Millions of people in all quarters of the world believe in it, and many have seen the thing called will-o'-the-wisp, but not necessarily in graveyards. I saw it once myself. I was riding a horse through a dark patch of woods, and the weird thing came out from the underbrush and shot across the road right in front of my horse. He shied horribly and almost threw me."

"What did it look like, Margot?" Gene was trying vainly to make his own deductions.

"Like nothing I'd ever seen before. It was like a small, live thing, made of fire, or charged with electricity. It rolled and danced its way along, keeping close to the ground. The encyclopedias admit that dead animal and vegetable matter exhales a phosphorescent glow under certain conditions. They are not sure that it ever seeps up from a coffin, through several feet of tightly-packed earth, but they don't deny the possibility."

"Anything's possible, I suppose," muttered Hart. "I'm just coming to that conclusion. Well, go on, Miss Anstruther. You've certainly got me guessing."

"A great French writer once said that 'he who pronounces a thing impossible, commits an imprudence,' so you're playing safe, Mr. Hart," she said with a laugh. "Of course, all great mysteries raise the question, 'Can such things be?' I fully believe that, within the bounds of physical law, unproved and amazing phenomena may occur. And I believe that the light that flickered on this floor—the one Boyle saw—was a will-o'-the-wisp, from the severed arm of Stella Ball."

Everyone stared at her, and Boyle heaved a great sigh of relief. It was as if her explanation had dispelled the shadow of the supernatural, which was all that concerned or interested him. Then Quinlan, as superstitious as Boyle, but with a quicker mind, or a more practical one, asked a question which Margot had expected to come from Hart.

"What about the hand that doused the flame, Miss?"

"Oh, that's quite simple. It was the hand of a person very much alive and, I believe, dangerous."

"Came to that conclusion myself," said Hart. Well, well, she thought, for the third time, Hart wasn't at all a fool. Then he asked her sharply: "Whose hand? Have you got that far?"

"Sure, if she could tell you that, Chief, the Mayor ought to make her Police Commissioner!" Quinlan's sarcasm was heavy, but it amused Margot.

"The hand," she began solemnly, "was the hand of the man Murchison, who stole the radium in the first place, and who is, in my opinion, the only major criminal in the whole affair."

"Sure, it was the old devil," Stella agreed eagerly. "Just like the old crook to come snoopin' round. He couldn't bear to lose it. But how the hell did he get in here without your seein' him?"

No one objected to the girl's swearing. It seemed rather to give vent to the general sentiment.

"Yes, how?" Hart was frowning again. "You don't mean you think he was in the room while you were in bed, and while Boyle was watching later? Where could he have hidden, I'd like to know?"

"Just a *minute!*" Margot couldn't control a low laugh at Hart's impatience. "Murchison was *not* in this room. If he *had* been he'd have been caught. But his *hand* was! Look! I'll show you."

She pointed to the small register with its iron grill-work, a few inches above the level of the floor, in the wall against which the head of the bed had stood. Mrs. Bellew, up to that moment obediently silent and motionless in her corner, came across the room with dilated eyes. She stood, as did the others, staring at the spot indicated by Margot, who was asking Hart to test it and telling him that he would find it loose. Murchison, she asserted, had loosened it.

"Do you see?" she said eagerly. "The hole's big enough to let through a hand and arm. It would be quite possible for a long arm to reach to the spot where the lights appeared."

"And it's a long arm he had. I remember it well!" Mrs. Bellew could no longer keep silent.

Hart fumbled with the grill-work. It gave way under his fingers and slid to one side. A dark hole gaped in the wall.

"I'll be damned if you're not right!" Hart exploded. "But I still don't get the part about the lights." He stood up and stared at Margot inquiringly.

"It's like this, Mr. Hart. Murchison has been tunneling through from the adjoining house. I calculate that he'd almost finished his job the night the trouble started—trouble for me, I mean," she added with a laugh. "Of course it's been awfully slow work. Once he got the grill loosened, he was able to reach in and suppress the lights on the rug—over and over again. He must have thought that the light from my match was like the others he'd seen. The point is, he couldn't risk letting *any* flame or light, call attention to the secret chamber underneath."

"Fine!" Hart's thin face glowed with satisfaction and understanding. "But there's just one thing, Miss Anstruther, which I don't get. Why didn't Murchison pick some quiet afternoon when he could have felt fairly sure the room wasn't occupied, and sneak in by the roof, the way the girl did?"

"I think I've checked up on that," Margot said quietly. She turned to the landlady. "Isn't it a fact, Mrs. Bellew, that between Stella's tenancy and mine, this room was occupied by two women?"

"Yes, dearie, a couple of cranky old maids they were, hipped on the subject of thieves breaking in and stealing their valuables, although I never could see what they had that anybody'd want."

"So one or the other of these women was always in the room? Is that right?"

"You're right, Miss Anstruther. It was that roof they were most scared of. They wouldn't trust no locks or bars."

Margot turned shining eyes to Hart. "Isn't that your answer?" she asked him eagerly. "Aren't you convinced?"

"I sure am." His dry, inexpressive face showed a degree of enthusiasm that flattered Margot more subtly than his admiring: "There aren't many detectives on the Force as good as you are, Miss Anstruther. I'm here to tell the world that!"

"I don't believe, Hart, that you've got one quite so good!" Gene's eulogy was accompanied by a glance of such mute admiration that Margot had to stifle a mad desire to run to him and throw her arms around his neck, regardless of her audience.

Then the natural-born pessimist in Hart came to the front.

"It's too bad," he said gloomily, "that we didn't have this information three days ago. The old fellow's had plenty of time to make his getaway. He won't be easy to find."

"You may be right, but my opinion of Murchison is that he simply couldn't tear himself away and leave that radium behind."

"You're right, Miss!" Stella once more became articulate.

"I'm almost sure he's still living right next door. He wouldn't start tunneling till late at night. I suggest that you go and take a look." She pointed to the wall.

"Ask whoever owns the house next door to let you examine the room corresponding to this one."

Hart, full of doubts, but ready by now to follow any lead suggested by Margot, marshaled his men, and departed, taking Stella with him. Before they left the room, Margot went up to Stella, and put her hand with a kindly pressure on the girl's thin shoulder.

"My dear," she said softly, "I don't know anything about you; where you came from, or what. But I do believe that you've been more sinned against than sinning, from the very beginning— whatever that beginning was. Perhaps you'll tell me some day. In the meantime, my dear, try to believe in my sincere sympathy. I'm going to stand by you and see that you get a square deal, first and last. I don't mean merely the trial which I'm afraid you'll have to stand. I mean *after* that. I'm going to help you every way I can—a good job, a decent home, all the rest of it."

She took Stella's left hand in hers and gave it a little squeeze. She smiled into her eyes—eyes as naturally distrustful as a cat's, but into which came a quivering light of gratitude and animal affection such as a child feels for those who give it tenderness and love. The beauty of trust and tenderness in Margot's lovely face, had conquered the girl's ugly spirit.

Margot dismissed or rather escaped the landlady and her inevitable bombardment of questions and excited conjectures by telling her that her head ached from the long strain, and that she must rest, then go for a walk and fresh air. In her room upstairs, to which she had beckoned Gene, she dropped wearily into an armchair, let him light a cigarette for her, and closed her eyes, slowly inhaling and blowing the smoke out from her parted lips. Gene sat quite still, smoking and watching her, but venturing no word nor caress. It was the most complete demonstration he could have made, of unity with her, and intelligent devotion.

When Margot finally opened her eyes and looked at him, she said softly:

"Gene, dear, I didn't realize what a brick you are—just the *kind* of a brick I like best," she added with one of her humorous twists to common-place things, and a twinkle in her gray eyes.

"You flatter me," he said smiling, but not moving from his chair. Again she was astonished at his understanding of her. She wasn't quite ready for any demonstrative expression of his feeling for her, and he knew it. Suddenly she felt that she would be ready for it sooner than she had supposed possible.

"The thing I like best," she went on, "is that you've let me rest here, and haven't asked me a single question, and all the time I know you've just been seething with a desire to ask one *particular* question, 'ain't it the truth?'" She laughed at the surprised widening of his eyes.

"If you know that much, I won't have to ask it," he said, his smile warming to a grin of appreciation of her quick wit.

"Question and answer—I'll supply both. You're wondering if I have the least idea, or rather an *opinion,* as to who the man was who came with Murchison the night Stella was injured. Well, my dear old scout, I certainly have—more than either an idea or an opinion. I've got a life-sized conviction—otherwise known as a *hunch!*"

"And *I'm* thinking," Gene said quickly, "that either I'm reading your mind with uncanny ease, or else I'm more of a sleuth than I supposed, for I know whom you mean—your mystery-man, with the pale eyes—your Superfilm director, Frederick Stoner."

"By jove!" she said with boyish eagerness. "You certainly are getting on! I'm thrilled, I'm proud of you, Gene!"

"Well, I've gotten that far, but I'm damned if I see just how he's been actually mixed up in it, except that I've followed your deductions pretty closely, and perhaps thought transference had something to do with it. I knew you meant Stoner, and that's all I do know."

"Didn't his picture, *The Masque of Life,* give you a clue—I mean something more than your first wrong guess about the powers of radium?"

"Certainly! The impression was vague at first, but afterwards, when I listened to some of the things you brought out, I made sense out of two things: Stoner's evident knowledge, superficial though it might be—of radium, and his attitude from the beginning, of being so eager to have you drop the mystery. Those two things seem to join up in my mind to indicate that Stoner must have had some connection with the theft of the radium. Is that what you mean, Margot?"

"No, not that he was involved in the theft of it. He would be too cautious for anything like that, and besides, impossible as he is in some ways, he's *not* a crook, whether from lack of nerve or inclination, I don't know. I'll give you another guess," she challenged him.

"My mind's a blank. Go on, dear. My curiosity threatens to overpower me."

"Well—here's the dope, as Stella Ball would put it. For days my suspicion regarding Stoner has been growing. That picture merely confirmed it. I felt instinctively that his *blah* about publicity was just that—blah—bunk. I knew that he was afraid of *something*. It was for his own sake, not mine, that he wanted me to drop the case. That meant he had something to conceal. And then, don't forget that queer look I used to see in his eyes, every now and then. The look I first noticed when I gave this house as my address. But still I was vague as to the real motive back of it all."

"And that picture supplied the missing link of cause and effect?" Gene asked with quick grasp of her chain of thought.

"Righto! That first, then Stella's story about the mysterious 'fat man,' who didn't want to buy the radium but only *rent* it. Now *why* would a movie director want to rent radium from a crook? Again, answer and question, both supplied while you wait." Her laugh was infectious. "Now listen carefully, old dear. Stoner's of the old school—full of notions about impressing the poor, long-suffering public, with the wildest sort of hokum. And he's rather ignorant, outside of his business. What he knew about things such as radium, you could stuff into a thimble."

"I get you," Gene interrupted eagerly. "That radium machine in the picture! He must have been working on that picture just at the time Stella disappeared. He got to a certain point, then he was stumped,—couldn't get the effects he wanted, so he decided to try to get hold of some radium. Must have read about the theft from the Fellowe Institute, but how the devil did he tie up with Murchison?"

"That's something we may or may not find out. All depends on what we *do* with Stoner." Again she laughed, overcome with humor at remembrance of Stoner's weak attempts to fake radium. "Wasn't it *funny* the way he made that diabolical machine glow in the dark, and shoot out rays like forked lightning? He must have thought that it had those properties. About as much like *radium* as mud! But how sore he must have been, with his bug about realism, when events forced him to get his effects by hoakum, and rotten hoakum at that!"

"Speaking of 'hoakum,' may I be permitted, my dear girl, to outrage your feelings by applying just that word to most of your eloquence on the subject of 'ignis fatuus'—'corpse candle'—'will-o'-the-wisp'—whatever it's called?" Gene grinned at her teasingly.

"You'd outrage my *intelligence*—and your own—if you didn't regard my eloquence on the subject in just that light. Of course there's more than a grain of truth as to the unproved yet undeniable possibilities regarding the phosphorescence from dead animal and vegetable matter. But in this case I skimmed lightly over thin ice—weak logic—in certain places."

"Notably," Gene interjected quickly, "in your ignoring of the fact that if the desiccated arm had been preserved from decay by heat and dryness, no exhaling of phosphorescence would be possible. I had to laugh at the way Hart swallowed whole all you said."

"Perhaps he didn't, really, but he seemed to. He'd been so darn skeptical, that when finally I got him on the run in my exposition of events, and he was eating right out of my hand, I couldn't resist the temptation to see how far I could go. Besides,

Gene, I think my imagination took the bit in its teeth. I almost believed what I was saying, once I'd started."

"Briefly, as I see it, Margot, the light you saw was a match, and Boyle, with his superstitious fears, might have seen anything, and you don't actually *know* that there *were* any lights at any time, for Murchison to tap out. Isn't that it?"

"Certainly. The night I got the scare, undoubtedly he saw my match and thought it safer to put it out while waiting for a propitious moment for what he planned to do."

"Well, to return to Stoner. I can't see why you're in doubt as to what to do with *that* bird."

"Just because, dear, Stoner's more of a fool than a knave, in my humble opinion. If Murchison is caught—which I'm sure he'll be—and if Murchison squeals, as they call it, on Stoner—which I'm not so sure of, for rogues sometimes have strange spasms of honor—then of course he could be punished for trafficking in stolen goods. But *I'm* not going to be the one to denounce him to the police. After all, he hasn't committed a *crime*."

"Good Lord! You're not going to let him go scot free!"

"No—not exactly." The smile on Margot's lips was a trifle feline in quality. "I have a subtle revenge and punishment planned, which I'm going to start going to-morrow. My unseen weapon is to be Corinne Delamar. Can't you picture the rumpus she'll start? First a personal one with her quondam lover, then one staged on a larger scale with the entire Superfilm organization as props, actors and camera men."

"By George, Margot! You'd have been invaluable to the subtle gentlemen at the time of the Inquisition!"

"Not quite so bad as that, am I?" She asked, laughing.

She read his answer in his eyes, and his sudden spring from his chair, as he came toward her. At that most inopportune moment—her heart said it was inopportune—the telephone rang. She had had a connection put in her new quarters. She ran to the instrument, brushing by Gene's out-stretched arms, and took up the receiver.

"Hello! Yes . . . yes . . . Fine! All right!" He heard her call into the mouthpiece, then she turned to him, and seized his arm excitedly.

"They've arrested Murchison!"

CHAPTER XIV

LOVE'S ALARM

Cornelius Hart surprised and delighted Margot with his unsuspected power for dramatic narrative. It was almost as exciting, she told him sweetly, as if she had been present at the pursuit, discovery, and final capture of Murchison.

". . . and so, after we'd smashed in his door, and searched everywhere in his almost empty room, I knew there was only one place he could be. He'd locked himself into the room, for the lodging-house woman next door was positive she'd seen him go up a short time before. She was equally sure he hadn't come down again. Funny, the way those dames keep track of their lodgers!" The amused reflection cut into his narrative.

"Yes, isn't it!" Margot laughed, with a sudden picture of her own landlady snooping around in halls and outside of doors.

"Well, as I was saying, I knew he was inside that room. There was no roof, like outside that room of yours, for him to get out on and no fire-escape either. I took one look at the hole he'd dug to get into this house, and I had a pretty good hunch where the old fellow was hiding. So we poked into it. I'll be damned if he hadn't crawled so far in, and was so tightly wedged in the tunnel, that it took two of us to drag him out by his heels."

"Poor old thing, I'm a little sorry for him, after all." Margot's tender heart was not proof even against the menace of a criminal who might have threatened her own safety.

"Don't waste your pity, Miss Anstruther! He's a hard old nut. But I'll say this much for him—he didn't squeal on the man involved with him the night the girl had her arm chopped off."

"I didn't think he would," Margot said, smiling at Gene. "Honor among thieves, Mr. Hart."

"He may tell yet. We haven't grilled him yet. Wait till he's brought to trial. That'll be the test, when he'll have a chance to get off light by squealing."

"Rotten ethics, I should say!" Margot's lips curled with scorn for the strange and devious ways of the law and of what is called justice.

"Well, that's the way it's always been, and always will be, I guess. Of course you'll have to be present at the trial, Miss Anstruther." He looked at her as if expecting a feminine protest, but Margot only laughed.

"I wouldn't miss it for the world! And besides," she added seriously, "I'm sincerely interested in that poor girl, so I'd want to be on hand for her sake, even if I didn't have to be."

When Hart had gone, Margot stared thoughtfully at Gene.

"I do hope," she said anxiously, "that I'll be able to get a light sentence for that poor girl. Wish I could get her off altogether, but I'm afraid there's no hope for that."

"Guess not. But if *anyone* can influence the judge in her favor, you can, Margot, in the circumstances. Shouldn't be surprised if she'd go straight after this, if they give her half a chance."

"I'm *sure* of it. She's got a real brain in that small head of hers, but she's had a rotten run for her money all her young life. 'Nous allons changer tout cela', as the French say. But my *next* job is to tackle our friend Stoner, through Corinne. And then—well, there'll be time for another matter of importance before the trial."

"Now what the devil have you up your sleeve?" Gene frowned impatiently.

"Oh, a most important and thrilling affair that will demand all my thought and time—for a few weeks."

Gene's despair was obvious. It would appear that the mystery, apparently cleared up, had fallen again. Apparently Margot was not yet ready to give him—and his love for her—their due place in the scheme of things.

"Don't you wish you knew?" she teased him. "All in good time, old dear."

"But, Margot, there's a limit to my endurance. I'm madly in love with you, and you promised to face that particular tragedy—and it most certainly is a tragedy for me until I can end this suspense—as soon as you cleared up the mystery. Now it's cleared up, and you actually have the nerve to tell me that when you've cleaned up Delamar and Stoner, you've still got another important matter to adjust!"

"I did say that, didn't I?" Her eyes tried to look dreamily absent, in a mist of uncertainty, but she couldn't prevent the spark ot laughter and roguish dart of mischief as her glance met his.

"You *are* a little devil!" He made a rush at her, but she was too quick for him.

"Come on, now, Gene! I'm famished and I'm sure you are too. Let's celebrate with a *good* dinner somewhere which includes the privilege of buying as many cocktails as we can swallow. I feel just like it, and I know just the place. Come on!"

Cocktails and dinner and jazz! It was the cheeriest, jolliest evening Margot had enjoyed since, the night of her now famous party. The late editions of the evening papers gave a grotesquely lurid account of the arrest of Murchison and of the events leading up to it, events in which Margot Anstruther, the beautiful and clever young screen star—a star, mind you!—had played the role of detective in the most thrilling of mystery stories since the time of Sherlock Holmes. Some particularly enterprising reporter had got hold of a picture of Margot—a "still" from the studio—in the costume of "Conchita." The morning papers would of course have additional details—most of them Simon Pure inventions, unless she interviewed the reporters, which she did, later in the evening, before going home.

Margot and Gene took bets as to what Stoner would do on reading the news about Murchison and the stolen radium. Gene bet that he would give himself away by his consciousness of guilt. Margot believed that he would bluff it out, and would try to get word to Murchison, to attempt to bribe the old man not to drag him into it.

"Of course," Margot said, "he's been on pins and needles for fear I'd unearth something. But now that the story of the radium and Stella's arm has come out, and Stoner's name hasn't been remotely referred to, I think he'll feel quite safe except for Murchison. You wait and see if I'm not right."

"As you've been right about everything else to date, I'll take your word for it, Margot."

She refused throughout the evening to talk about herself. When Gene took her home, she let him go into her room to smoke a cigarette, but love-making seemed to be taboo. She was tired, she was nervous, she was sleepy—any one of the hundred things a woman can be when she doesn't want a man's caresses. Finally Gene, baffled and a little resentful, rose to go.

He bent over her, his eager eyes and lips demanding at least a good-night kiss. She rose slowly and put both hands on his shoulders, looking him squarely in the eyes, without the suspicion of a smile. She said solemnly:

"You may kiss me good night, Gene—as a *brother*. It may be for the very last time," with which vague threat she kissed him herself, on the lips, in a frankly sisterly manner, and she laughed suddenly into his puzzled eyes.

Puzzlement changed quickly to resentment. She saw his eyes darken and flash, and his lips tighten. He drew back and shook off her hands from his shoulders. Then he said quietly:

"You're making a fool of me, Margot, and I don't particularly relish it. If my love for you strikes you merely as a joke, Or something to be sisterly about, it's time I got out from under. I'm getting a little tired of mysteries and of a game which amuses only one of us."

Surprised, then suddenly angry at his impatience and failure to respond to her mood, Margot spoke coldly.

"Your remark about getting out from under would seem to imply that I've been trying to *hold* you. That's a little far-fetched, isn't it, Gene?"

He took a step nearer to her, his eyes glowing with suddenly released passion. With a sweep of his arm he seized her and crushed her against him. He bent his head and kissed her eyes and then her mouth as he had never dared to kiss her before. She was too startled to struggle in his arms, and as suddenly as he had seized her he let her go. His lips, trembling from their passionate contact with hers, formed words that tumbled brokenly, one over the other.

"*That's*—just how—*brotherly*—I feel—for you. That's the way—I'm going to kiss you—if at all. I'll never kiss you again—I'll never *see* you—again—unless you send for me—to be your husband—or your lover." He seemed to fling the last word at her in bitter defiance.

"Your—technique—hasn't improved." She knew that it had, but she said that, urged by a vague, primitive desire to see what he would do if further exasperated. She might have known that he would take her a little too literally.

"No," he said, with slow bitterness. "I don't suppose it has," and with that, and before she could detain him with a word or look, he tore open her door and slammed it behind him.

Silly—silly, of them both, Margot reflected, as she undressed. Of course Gene would get over his extraordinary burst of angry resentment, and, of course, when he understood just what she had meant by saying that he could give her a brotherly kiss for the last time, he would be sorry he had been so fierce. However, it was rather interesting and exciting to find that Gene *could* be fierce like that.

She touched her lips softly, still feeling the pressure of his. She smiled and a little thrill of genuine emotion made her tremble. For the first time in several nights, Margot slept the dreamless sleep of a happy, healthy girl who is in love with life and in love with a man. Gene's outburst had made very clear to her that she loved him. She would call him back, oh, yes, nothing would be easier, but she would wait until. . . . Into unconsciousness she carried the vision of his face with its dark, flashing eyes, and the touch of his lips on hers.

CHAPTER XV

STONER'S SHARE

Margot made an early start for Astoria. Her impatience to talk with Corinne Delamar would have brought her to the studio still earlier if there had been any hope of finding the star on the lot before eleven o'clock. Very different, this voluntary call upon Corinne, to Margot's last visit, solicited by the star and made by Margot with bored distaste. She laughed softly to herself, remembering her eavesdropping and the advantage it had given her over Stoner. It might be true that listeners never hear good of themselves, but at least it would appear that sometimes what they heard in this unapproved manner gave them the whip-handle in dealing with crooks, or, to be more charitable, those who followed crooked ways.

She went straight to Corinne's dressing-room. The colored maid said that her mistress was doing a scene a short distance from the studio, but would return in a half hour, she thought. Margot waited an hour, amusing herself with a movie periodical she found in the dressing-room. Among other diverting matter it contained an interview with Miss Delamar, which gave a word picture of the actress as a person of high ideals, strict views on love and marriage, and a belief that the moving picture industry was the greatest symbol of art for art's sake, and morality for the world, that had so far been discovered. Very clever of Corinne! And clever of the interviewer, who had carefully avoided the slightest suggestion of irony. That was the sort of thing the movie fans ate up, and what the moving-picture industry hoped that they would digest and thrive on. There was also a "still" of Corinne, which indicated a beauty as ravishing as it was pure and noble. Well, well! Margot wondered if she would ever have such a chance to laugh at a description of herself.

Corinne stood in the small doorway looking at Margot with curious but not antagonistic eyes. Margot rose quickly and asked her pardon for having taken the liberty of waiting for her in her dressing-room. She particularly did not wish to see anyone else, she carefully explained. Corinne, dressed as the heroine in *A Toreador's Love,* and looking prettier than usual—a purely fleshly prettiness—was gracious in a stilted way (the only way possible to her, when she felt socially inferior to another woman), told Margot please to sit down, and offered her a cigarette. Margot, remembering that her father had once told her that in any interview the first advantage lies with the one who speaks last, deliberately waited for Corinne to begin the conversation. Margot could be silent, with a beaming smile, and gentle repose of manner, most misleading to strangers.

"What can I do for you, Miss Anstruther?" That wasn't so stupid of Corinne, Margot thought, smiling sweetly, for it put her at once in the position of one dispensing patronage. Margot's smile became still more friendly and confidential.

"That's awfully nice of you, Miss Delamar, but you see, I've come to do something for *you!*" Corinne's cigarette hung loosely from her painted lips, as she stared at Margot.

"I don't quite see what *you* can do for *me,* Miss Anstruther—in the circumstances." Nasty dig that, thought Margot, still smiling.

"Nevertheless," she said gently, "I'm going to try to. And one of my reasons for doing so, Miss Delamar, is that I have always liked you." Naughty Margot! What more subtle way of patronizing than to assure an acquaintance that you've always liked them? Yet the genuine ring of friendliness in her voice made Corinne say quickly:

"And, as a matter of fact, I've liked you, although there seemed to be plenty of reason why I shouldn't."

"You're mistaken. There hasn't been any such reason— not for a moment." This time there was no doubt of Margot's sincerity.

"You mean—what you said the last time you were here— about having no particular use for Fred Stoner, in a personal way, I mean?"

"Yes, that, and all that stuff he filled your head with about my working publicity in order to get an advantage over you. What I told you that day—just the other day, but it seems ages ago—I've come here to-day to prove to you, Miss Delamar."

Corinne frowned, looking from Margot to the floor, out into space and back at Margot as if trying to piece together disconnected facts. Then she said:

"I don't know what you have to tell me, but I suppose it has something to do with your mystery story. Although I can't imagine how *that* can concern Stoner or me, now that you're no longer in the cast, Miss Anstruther."

"Did you read what the papers published last night and this morning?" Margot asked quickly.

"I read this morning's story. How much of it is true?"

"All of it! I got hold of some newspaper men last night, and made them agree to write it up for to-day's papers with some idea of sticking to facts. But of course there's a lot they didn't print because they know nothing about it. And it's *that* I've come here to tell you. You remember the reference to the fat man whom Stella Ball said had come to her room that night, with Murchison, offering to pay a certain sum for the rental for a week of the radium stolen by Murchison?"

"Yes. The one who is supposed to have paid the girl's hospital bill?" Corinne seemed to make no connection yet, in her mystified brain.

"Well, that fat man—as the girl described him—was—is—a would-be famous film director, by name Frederick Stoner!"

Corinne stared at her without speaking. The ashes from her cigarette fell over her breast, and she threw the cigarette into a corner of the room. Finally she said slowly:

"I suppose—Miss Anstruther—you wouldn't dare—make such a statement—without being able—to give proof?"

"Hardly!" Margot gave a short laugh, a hard little laugh, recalling Stoner's contemptible treatment of her and of Gene.

"What *is* your proof?"

"The 'proof' will speak for himself."

"You mean the man Murchison, but he's refused, the police say, to squeal on his customer, as he calls him. You mean you know that Murchison will give it away in court?"

"No, I don't mean that at all. I mean that the man himself— the one who was there *with* Murchison, will be the living proof, and to *you*, Miss Delamar."

Corinne studied her with narrowed, suspicious eyes. She seemed trying to take the measure of the quiet, self-contained girl who sat in front of her, throwing out vague hints, that perhaps weren't so vague after all. An expression flashed suddenly in her green eyes, which told Margot that Corinne's intelligence had risen to the occasion.

"I suppose you're insinuating, Miss Anstruther, that you've got enough on Fred Stoner to force his confession?"

"Precisely! And his confession to you in my presence, if you'll be so kind as to send for him. And just one thing more, before he comes. I don't believe that Stoner is always aboveboard in his affairs with women. I want to confess something myself. The other day, when you sent for me, I started to go to my dressing-room before seeing you. As I reached the foot of the stairs, I heard your voice talking about me. I felt no hesitancy in listening, after hearing my own name, in view of your sending for me and of the attitude Stoner had taken about my investigating the mystery of my room."

"Do you mean to say you heard the whole conversation?" Corinne's red lips trembled and her eyes darkened with anger.

"Hardly that, for I've no idea how long it was going on before I arrived. Also I ran off after I'd heard enough to prove what I'd already suspected, that he was trying his best to start something between you and me."

"You didn't hear anything—anything of a more—personal nature?"

"Personal, you mean, Miss Delamar, as between you and Stoner? I'm afraid I did. I heard enough to understand that you thought—as you implied to me in our *first* short interview— that I was flirting with him, and that he was interested in me. I heard also enough to know that he has either lied to you or lied to me or—as is quite as likely—lied to both of us. I heard him assure you of his loyal devotion, or something like that, and of his utter indifference to me. And I want to tell you, because I really like you, that his advances toward me, whatever his motives may have been, took the form of forced love-making in my room, when he had come unbidden, with the excuse of having a theory to give me about my mystery. And not only did he force his physical attentions, but he begged me to marry him, took away my job because I refused—incidentally I struck him across the face—because I lost my temper—and told me he'd give the job back to me any time I might decide to marry him."

Corinne had not interrupted by a word or a gesture, merely watching with eyes that glinted like a cat's. Then she said:

"I believe what you say, for if your statement about his being the man who wanted to rent the radium is true, then you can punish him enough in that direction without revenging yourself by lying about his asking you to marry him."

Margot, rather amazed by Corinne's ability to reason so logically, said eagerly:

"That's absolutely right. My only reason for telling you that part of the story which concerns Stoner and myself in a personal way, is because it concerns you also, in so much as I have reason to believe that you've felt an interest in Stoner which I'm afraid he doesn't appreciate. As one woman to another, I want to warn you."

In spite of the makeup on cheeks and lips, Corinne had turned very white. Margot felt a chill disgust, tempered by pity, that so pretty, and, she believed, decent a girl as Corinne, should have fallen for a man like Stoner. Corinne moistened her dry lips and called to her maid. She told her to find the director and tell him that Miss Delamar must see him at once on an urgent matter. Then she cautioned the maid, in no circumstances to let Stoner suspect that she had a caller in her dressing-room.

Corinne turned to her dressing-table, studied her face in the mirror, and carefully rubbed in some cold cream, rubbed it off, added a soft liquid powder, then a cream rouge on lips and cheeks, then a soft dusting of powder. Also she put some drops in her eyes. Then she forced a smile and told Margot that she was ready to receive the "would-be famous film director." Strange, Margot thought, that although Corinne had been loath to believe ill of Stoner when it concerned crooked outside dealings, she seemed to have accepted Margot's arraignment of him regarding their personal relations, without question!

Margot would never forget Stoner's expression when he stood just inside the small dressing-room, and met her amused and calmly accusing eyes. Corinne, watching him with her green eyes, did not miss the quick batting of his eyelids, the drawing in of his thick lips, and the yellowish film that covered, for an instant, the iris of his pale blue eyes, when his first glance discovered Margot sitting at ease in the star's dressing-room.

Again Margot conferred the disadvantage on her antagonist, by giving him the first chance to speak, and Corinne intuitively did the same. Stoner, his eyes half covered by his heavy lids, looked with surly assurance from one woman to the other. Instinctively he seemed to feel their alignment, and antagonism to him.

"What do you want?" he said with gruff abruptness, his expressionless eyes fixed on the star.

Before Corinne could answer him, Margot said quietly:

"*She* doesn't really want anything of you, Mr. Stoner. *I'm* the one who wants to see you." She held his eyes with a gaze so keen and masterful that his glance wavered and fell.

"I just wanted to tell you, Mr. Stoner, in the presence of Miss Delamar, that I know, beyond any possibility of doubt or denial on your part, that you were the man who went to the room of Stella Ball and who wanted to rent that radium!"

As if against his will, his eyes once more met Margot's. There was no mistaking that look of fear, followed swiftly by a gleam of anger.

"Hell of a lot you know about me!"

His language, though inelegant, made Margot smile in his face, which enraged him still further. He glared at her venomously.

"I was a fool to choose *you* that day, instead of Lulu Leinster."

Margot's irritating smile broadened.

"I believe I've heard you express those sentiments before, Mr. Stoner. In view of what I know about you, your reason for choosing me that day, for the picture, is quite obvious. I repeat my accusation about Stella Ball and the radium."

Stoner's face grew purple. "What the devil do you mean by telling such lies? Don't you know you can be sued for libel—defamation of character?" His threat held so much bluster that it made Margot smile again.

"Not by you, Mr. Stoner, for what I accuse you of isn't libel or defamation of character. It's God's truth. Quite apart from the way you aroused my suspicions by all that rot about publicity, and your evident eagerness to make me drop the matter of my mystery—not to mention a very strange expression I caught in your eyes several times, notably when I first gave you my address; your behavior the night you called on me (your call was merely a ruse to examine that room), your extraordinary antics in the room where the policeman was keeping guard, and your still more extraordinary and utterly unconvincing theory about the lights and the hand putting them out—merely an attempt to choke off my theories, or an excuse for your call; all this set the stage beautifully for the final curtain." She stopped, watching him with amusement overlaying her serious intent to corner him.

"What do you mean?" Sheer curiosity forced the quick question.

"I mean, Mr. Stoner, the remarkable kick I got out of your picture *The Masque of Life,* with its weird and absurd portrayal of the magic properties of radium!"

She saw his lips twitch and his pale eyes grow darker as the pupils dilated. She knew that what she saw, Corinne must also see, but she would not shift her glance from Stoner's self-accusing face.

"I'm a damn fool to stand here talking to you," he said, wetting his lips. "But since you've started things, you might as well finish. What in all creation has that picture got to do with that girl Stella and the man Murchison?"

"Everything in creation," Margot said, smiling. "I'm not accusing you of having a thing to do with the *theft* of the radium, Mr. Stoner, but I do assert that when you wanted to get more realism into your picture, you thought it would be a fine idea to get hold of some radium. I haven't *yet* mastered all the details of your acquaintance with Murchison, but I know beyond all doubt, that you tried your best to get the radium *he'd* stolen, *knowing* he'd stolen it, which of course, makes you an accessory after the crime, Mr. Stoner."

He worked his mouth into a twisted, scornful smile, as he said threateningly:

"You just try, young lady, making any public charge like the one you've just made."

"She won't have to! *I'll* do the charging—to our board of directors!" Corinne stood up and glared into his astonished eyes.

Surprise changed to insensate rage as he stared back at his star.

"You will, will you! Well, you just try it, and see where *you* get off!"

"Oh," she said calmly, "I expect to get off very well, thank you.

I expect to get a new director for our company who won't have to consort with crooks in order to put on pictures and make himself famous."

"You're crazy!" He looked a little that way himself, as his lips and hands worked convulsively. "What do you think you can prove of this girl's wild story? Nothing—absolutely nothing!"

"Oh, yes she can, Mr. Stoner." Margot's voice had velvet in it, and her smile was sweeter than ever. "You seem to have forgotten that the girl Stella Ball, although deprived of one arm, thanks to the quarrel between you and Murchison, still has the perfect use of her eyes—both of them. She says she could pick you out anywhere, at a single glance. She'll never forget you, she says."

Lie, little Margot, lie in a good cause! Why not! It was a good and a safe card to play, for without doubt Stella *would* recognize Stoner at a glance, even if she failed to describe him accurately. And the wild shot went straight home. Stoner seemed to crumble, morally, right before their eyes. Margot, quick to follow up an advantage, went on with quiet assurance.

"You see, Mr. Stoner, you can do one of three things. You're really lucky to have so much to choose from, and you really owe that to me. You can make a break for the open; get out while the getting's still good, prove—to our satisfaction—your guilt beyond question, but escape, perhaps, its penalty. Or you can face your board of directors and deny my accusations, which will enable *me* to prove them to *everyone's* satisfaction. Or—and permit me to suggest that this last would be your wisest course—you can admit the facts to your board of directors, plead clemency, which Miss Delamar and I will also plead for you, take what's coming to you, so far as getting out of this company is concerned, and escape the penalty of the law, also the ignominy of having other film companies hear the truth about you. I'm sure that if you make it easy for everyone concerned, your board of directors will agree to keep the story from spreading."

Corinne's large and expressive eyes stared at Margot with an admiration as sincere as it was obvious. Then the star turned a haughty glance of dismissal at Stoner.

"That's about all, Fred Stoner, except that I'd like to tell you that I'm fully aware of all the lies you've told me, first and last, and if I do agree to do what Miss Anstruther suggests, and ask the Board to give you clemency, I want you to understand that it will be because I'd be afraid that otherwise, your vast and ridiculous conceit would imagine I was trying to wreak vengeance on you for personal reasons. And now, please go!"

He went—without another word—and Margot returned in full measure, the admiration Corinne had given her.

"That was very, very clever of you," she said earnestly. "That last remark, I mean. I think that between us, Miss Delamar, we've been just a little too much for the gentleman."

"Gentleman!" Corinne's scorn lay too deep for humor or irony.

"Just a form of speech, my dear. And now let me tell you how very glad I am that you and I are going to be friends, as of course we shall be after this. And, by the way, could you fix it up so that I can be present at the meeting of the board of directors?"

"Certainly," Corinne said warmly. "I wouldn't miss having you there. In fact, it's quite necessary that you should be. And I am glad too that we can be friends. And I'm grateful to you for showing me what an awful fool I've been for taking any stock in that man, or anything that he's ever said to me."

"Oh, I didn't mean it that way," Margot said hastily. "I don't, think you've been a fool at all, but I didn't want to see you in danger of being put in a false position."

"Very nice of you to put it that way. Well, good-by!" And she took Margot's outstretched hand in a friendly clasp of good-fellowship and trust.

And that was that, as Margot said to herself, with her ironic and characteristic manner of disposing of a situation or a problem.

CHAPTER XVI

A KING'S RANSOM IN RADIUM

A telegram from Corinne Delamar, later in the day, advised Margot that the strategically planned directors' meeting was to take place the following morning at eleven, and would Margot please be on hand without fail. Not that Corinne so described the meeting, but Margot knew her well enough by this time, to be sure of the strategy implied.

She decided to telephone Gene to ask him to come to see her the following evening. For the moment she was weary of discussion and analysis, and not in the mood for an interview with Gene which was likely to be rather strenuous, everything considered. Besides, she would prefer to clean up her "job" as amateur detective—dispose finally of Stoner—before coming to an understanding with Gene. It did not occur to her that he might be sulking, or that he could be anything but eager to answer her summons.

Her telephone call brought no response. Strange, because Gene was invariably in his room at that hour, waiting for a call from her. She rang his number twice more before going to bed. She wondered where he could be, and a vague uneasiness possessed her. Could he actually be angry with her to the point of not answering the phone? Funny old Gene! Well, she'd explain things to-morrow night.

The next morning she met Corinne in her dressing-room. It was getting to be a habit, Margot told the star, with her customary whimsicality.

"Funny, isn't it!" Corinne laughed, making Margot welcome. "If anybody'd told me a week ago that you and I would be getting chummy about anything under the shining sun—Stoner least of all—I'd have told them to go to an alienist. But here we are, actually in cahoots to see that our friend gets his just deserts." She offered her guest a cigarette, then lighted it for her, adding: "And the funniest part of the whole thing is that I'm not a bit unhappy about it. It was a shock at first, but that's all. I find I'm not really one little bit in love with Stoner, and I thought I was, you know."

"I'm mighty glad you're not!" Margot said earnestly. "He isn't fit to clean your shoes, Miss Delamar."

"He never would have." Corinne looked down at her shoes and laughed contemptuously. "He's the kind who, after a few months of marriage, would let his wife clean *his* shoes. It's strange, once you begin shedding your illusions about a person, how clearly you see every fault."

"Too clearly, I think," Margot said thoughtfully. "If you've begun by exaggerating a person's good points, when you begin to wake up you almost always exaggerate the bad points. I'm quite sure that no man is ever as good as the woman who loves him believes him to be, and never as bad as the woman who hates him considers him to be. It's the same the other way round."

"You're some little philosopher, aren't you, Miss Anstruther? No wonder you ferreted out Stoner's connection with your mystery. You're awfully clever. I wish I were!"

"If it's that bad," laughed Margot, "I'll have to become a little *more* clever and disguise the fact that I *am* clever. Clever girls aren't popular, you know."

"Well, *you're* popular, so there must be exceptions." There was no mistaking Corinne's sincerity. She was not simply flattering Margot, with or without design.

"Everyone here has been awfully kind to me." It was so trite a remark that Margot chuckled inwardly at her concession to the commonplace.

Corinne glanced at her watch. "About ten minutes more, then we'll have to go to the board room. Won't it be amusing seeing Stoner make a fool of himself—as of course he will, trying to worm himself out of the corner we've got him in!"

"Does he know about this directors' meeting?"

"He does not," said Corinne with a vicious little dab at her nose with her powder pad. "Or rather, if he's heard about it it's by snooping round, for he hasn't been officially notified. You see"—she gave a sudden laugh—"the directors don't know themselves. I didn't want anything to leak out, so I merely sent a note to our manager, Marx Klein, saying that there was something of the utmost importance which I wished to take up with the board of directors to-day, and would he please call a meeting. He sent back word that he would."

"You've certainly got the power to make them sit up and take notice, Miss Delamar." Margot smiled with frank approval.

"I've got my nerve, perhaps you mean, but it's this way. When you get to be a star, you can have as much 'temperament' as you like. They don't dare squelch it. So when I ask for anything special, they take for granted that a refusal will mean some kind of a blow-out on my part, and they don't dare risk it. I've never asked for a board meeting *before,* so they're sure it's something out of the ordinary."

"Which it certainly is," laughed Margot.

"Well—at least it will mean the official removal of Stoner's fat head. A sore head it'll be before we get through with him."

A tap on the door, and the black face of Corinne's maid, with bright, bulging eyes, whispering to her mistress that the director would like to have a few minutes' conversation with her. Could he come in?

"Now, what the devil!" Corinne scowled, looking from the maid to Margot.

"Do you suppose he's come to beg for mercy?" Margot whispered.

"A lot of good it'll do him! Shall we see him or not?" She seemed to depend on Margot's judgment.

"I think we might as well," Margot said thoughtfully. "It's always as well to hear whatever your enemy—or your victim"— she suppressed a giggle—"has to say for himself."

"All right. Tell him to come in," Corinne said to the maid.

Stoner stepped into the small inclosure. If the girls had expected to see a browbeaten, anxious or suppliant Frederick Stoner, they were disappointed. His shoulders were straight, his head erect, and his eyes clear and direct in their gaze, first at one girl, then at the other. In sheer astonishment at his expression and attitude, Corinne kept silence. Her face showed her surprise, but Margot's expression was not so easy to read. She wondered if he'd come with any sort of a threat up his sleeve. It would serve no purpose if so.

"Well," he said, slowly. "I hear a board meeting is to take place shortly. I heard of it last night. I've got something to say to you two. I'm not a fool, whatever else you may think me, and I know damn well that I gave myself away in this very room, yesterday." He looked at Margot as he spoke.

"You certainly did," she said quickly.

"But that wouldn't cut much ice, Miss Anstruther, if you didn't have the goods on me in the person of that skinny little thing, Stella Ball." Again he paused and stared at her.

Humph! That impromptu shot of hers had certainly gone home! It was a good shot, anyway. A legitimate shot! She said quietly:

"Of course I knew, Mr. Stoner, that you were intelligent enough to realize just what Stella Ball's recognition of you and testimony would mean."

"Right. But if I'd been smart enough to bluff you out on your deductions, and all that tripe that didn't and couldn't *prove* anything, you'd probably never have thought of the Stella end of it."

Margot merely smiled, but her instant thought was that he had more logic than she had supposed.

"Did you come here now just for the pleasure of telling us what we know already—that we've got the goods on you?" Corinne's voice rasped sharply and baneful yellow lights shone in her green eyes.

"No, I didn't," Stoner snapped at her. "I'll tell you what I came for. To tell you that you won't have the satisfaction of making a fool of me before any company directors." He turned to look again at Margot. "I decided last night to choose an alternative *not* suggested by you. I'm going to get out while the getting's good, but I'm not *sneaking* out. And, by the way, Miss Anstruther, you may be interested to hear that the lovely Lulu is coming out there too."

Corinne gave a start, and her eyes drew together in a quick frown as she stared at Stoner. There was something in his smile that suggested malice.

"Why should I be interested particularly in Lulu's plans?" Margot asked the question with cool impudence because his smile affected her unpleasantly.

He shrugged one shoulder. "Thought you'd be glad to know she's getting out of your way."

"Out of *my* way!" Irritation gave way to astonishment. "Just what do you mean by that, Mr. Stoner?"

"We—ll—" He rubbed the back of his head in affected embarrassment. "Valery, you know. Thought you'd be glad to have her out of *his* way."

Margot regarded him with puzzled eyes, but Corinne's lips smiled sneeringly.

"What perfect rot!" she said disgustedly.

Stoner turned to her angrily. "Where do you come into this thing? Margot's no fool. She must know that Gene Valery is rushing the Leinster kid. Why, I saw them together at a night club, about one o'clock this morning."

"I believe you're lying." Corinne spoke with deceptive gentleness. "Just when, may I ask, did you engage Lulu to go out to the coast?"

"Oh—recently," Stoner said, indicating vagueness of time and space with a wave of his fat hand.

From narrowed eyes Corinne watched him, gave a low sound that suggested a grunt of contempt and disbelief, then turned a friendly glance upon Margot.

"Of course, Miss Anstruther, neither you nor I have the slightest interest in Lulu Leinster's movements. But we're very much interested in Stoner's. You say," she said sternly, looking at the director, "that you're getting out of here. Just when, may I ask?"

"Mailed my resignation to the president last night. He got it this morning. I don't know what you told them, but from what I gather, you merely asked to have a meeting called. Well, I've got a ticket and Pullman reservation to California" (he dug into his pocket, brought forth the tickets and swung them lightly in front of him). "I'm going straight to Hollywood. Made arrangements at that end by wire. I'm taking a train in about an hour, at the Penn station. As your idea seemed to be to get rid of me, I take it you'll be satisfied with the little plan I've made." His smile at Corinne was sardonic.

For a moment she was at loose ends. She threw a worried glance at Margot.

"You *did* tell him you wouldn't do anything to him if he'd get out, but what in God's name will I tell the directors, not to speak of Klein and the president, Joseph Livingstone."

"You can tell 'em anything you please!" Stoner spoke with sudden fierceness. "Spill *all* the beans, for all I care! They won't be able to get hold of me. Margot said she'd see that the matter'd be dropped if I'd admit to the directors that what she says is true, and leave the company. What's the use taking the president into your sweet confidence," his thick lips curled bitterly, "if it's on the books that he won't punish me? I'm going anyway, in five minutes, and nobody can stop me that I know of."

"I agree with Mr. Stoner," Margot said quietly. "Let him go as he plans to. Call off the meeting. They'll just think your temperament's working over-time." She gave Corinne a friendly little smile.

Deep puckers filled the space between Corinne's two, rather lovely, green eyes. Her mouth drew into a straight line, and she took a few nervous puffs at her cigarette. Then, surprisingly, the expression of anxious uncertainty changed to a sparkling of the eye, and a smile of almost childish satisfaction. She threw away her cigarette with a gesture as of having more vital matters to deal with.

"I know *just* what I'll say to the president and directors! It's come to me like a flash!"

Stoner studied her with dislike in his eyes.

"Don't try to spring anything that'll mean the breaking of Miss Anstruther's word to me!"

"Oh, *you!*" Contempt unspeakable in Corinne's face and voice. "I wasn't even *thinking* of you that minute!"

Blank amazement in Stoner's face and on Margot's. Then Stoner said, addressing Margot:

"I guess that's about all. As for you, Miss Anstruther, I believe you'll do exactly what you said you would—give me a chance to get out, and drop the case against me. You're too clever to be anything but square."

She looked at him thoughtfully. His remarks about Gene had obviously been inspired by jealous malice, and she was inclined to agree with Corinne that he had lied, although it seemed like rather a silly and superfluous lie. Well—time for Gene later. No use getting upset by anything Stoner said. So far as leaving without springing any new tricks on them was concerned, she decided that he was acting in good faith. Better let him go and drop everything, although what Corinne suddenly felt inspired to tell the directors she couldn't imagine. She addressed Stoner quietly.

"All right, Mr. Stoner. You can count on my word. Hollywood is a comfortably long ways off. You're wise in going there. But I'd like to ask you to tell me something before you go. Two questions. First, how did you first get in touch with Murchison? I'd like to know."

Stoner hesitated, then said slowly: "Might as well tell you. He came to me a year ago, with some stones he wanted to sell.

Heard I was staging a costume play, and offered me a ruby for such a nominal sum that it made me suspicious at once. I didn't want anything to do with stolen goods, and told him so, flat. He pulled a long, sad face, and a long, unconvincing story. Said a rich friend had died and left him the stones. Then he told me he was employed at the Fellowe Institute, and said I could call up and verify that fact. I told him I'd do that and then get in touch with him if I wanted to buy anything from him. So I called up the Institute, found he was employed there all right—their description of the old duck tallied with mine. But somehow that didn't convince me that he hadn't stolen those stones. It sounded phony and what he asked for them was ridiculous. Why, any jeweler would have given four times as much and I told him so. He said he didn't want to bother with jewelers. So I dropped the matter."

Stoner stopped to light a cigarette, and Margot said quickly:

"And when you read in the papers about the theft of the radium you remembered Murchison, and you had a hunch he'd taken it?"

"Right. But Murchison came to my mind in connection with radium, only because I got stumped trying to make a realistic scene in that picture of mine, *The Masque of Life*. So I looked him up, and at first he denied all knowledge of the radium. But I offered such a whacking price for it—I thought at first I wanted to buy, but decided that would be too dangerous, it was a veritable king's ransom in radium—that he weakened and admitted that he had it. The rest I guess you know."

"Second question, Mr. Stoner. What makes you suppose that you won't be brought back here from California, when Murchison's trial takes place, about six weeks from now? Are you so sure he won't peach on you?"

"Dead sure!" Stoner spoke with conviction. "I'll tell you why.

I arranged with Murchison in the beginning, that if anything happened about the radium and he got caught, if he'd agree to keep me out of it—never mention my name to a soul—I'd put ten thousand in the bank for him. And I'll do just that. In fact it's done. I made all arrangements the day after he was arrested. The minute the trial's over, if he's kept his mouth shut, he'll get notice that the money's in the bank in his name. If he squeals, he'll get nothing, and it won't do *him* any good to drag me into it. No matter what they could do to me, it wouldn't go easier with him for having dragged me into it. *He* stole the radium. I had nothing to do with that. He'll go up for that anyway, and a wad in the bank at his convenience, when he gets out of jail, won't be anything to sneeze at. So *that's* why I'm so sure I won't be dragged back from Hollywood—that is, if *you* play the game as I believe you will, Miss Anstruther."

"I'll play it just that way," she said quietly. "Good-by, Mr. Stoner. I advise your sticking to romance in the pictures you direct. It won't require the assistance of science to aid realism." The smile she gave him, although conveying a mocking taunt, was not unfriendly. He struck her suddenly as so much more a fool than a knave, even in his childishly malicious gossip about Gene.

Abruptly he stuck out his large hand. "Will you shake on it, Miss Anstruther, just to show there's no hard feeling?"

"Certainly!" She gave him her hand and he shook it with a great show of sexless cordiality. That was for Corinne's benefit.

He turned to go, without so much as a glance at Corinne. She said sharply:

"You're darn lucky you have to deal with a girl as square as Margot Anstruther. Even if I wanted to play you a mean trick, she wouldn't let me do it."

"Don't need to remind me," he said, with an ugly look at the star, "that you'd play me a dirty trick if you dared. But *she'll* see to that!" And the next instant the door closed behind him.

"Dirty dog!" It was Corinne's irrepressible but final disposal of the man for whom her love had turned to hate.

Margot, with her unquenchable sense of humor, said, with a smile she tried to keep from spreading into a roguish grin:

"That gives you the last word. Now forget him! He's really occupied more time and space in my young life than he's worth, except that he's furnished me with considerable amusement, first and last."

"Well, I don't see it—the amusement part. But, as you say, forget him! Only there's one little matter I'm not quite through with, that is about Lulu Leinster. I signed her up last week, for a part in my new picture. She may have played me a nasty trick, but I doubt it. I believe Stoner sprung that stuff about her going out to the coast, just to spite you, because you'd cornered him. I'm pretty sure it's a lie, and I'm dead sure the part about seeing her with Gene *was* a lie."

Margot moved restlessly. "That's of no importance, is it, but it is important whether she's broken her contract with you."

"I'll soon find out. I'll send for her to come here."

Corinne summoned her maid and directed that she request Miss Leinster to meet Miss Delamar in her dressing-room within a half hour.

"And now for the board meeting," she said cheerfully, rising. "We're late, of course, but they'll wait. Just watch them jump to their big flat feet, and bow and scrape as if I'd done them an honor by keeping them waiting."

"But, Miss Delamar," Margot hung back, "whatever your business is with the directors, you won't need *me* now."

"I most certainly will!" Corinne put her hand on Margot's arm, and pushed her toward the door. "Now, more than before, if you only knew!" And then she laughed into Margot's questioning eyes.

"But—I don't understand. You're going to drop the case of Stoner altogether, you said?"

"I am! But I didn't say I was going to drop *your* case, did I?"

Margot was puzzled. She didn't know Corinne well, after all. What on earth was she driving at? However, she, Margot, had nothing to conceal—except for the sake of her promise to Stoner—and her curiosity was aroused. Also she wasn't a quitter. If Corinne wanted her to *go* with her to that board meeting, why she'd go!

"You won't tell me why you want me to go with you," she temporized once more.

"You'll find out quick enough. Come on, please, Miss Anstruther! Have a heart and don't let us keep the poor things waiting any longer!"

So they hurried—until they reached the door of the board room. Then Corinne put on her most nonchalant manner, and walked into the room as if royalty itself had arrived with, as it were, a blowing of silver trumpets and a tinkling of silver bells. Even Margot was impressed, not by the star's importance, but by the way she got away with it. Every man in the room rose to his feet, bowing obsequiously, with broad and admiring smiles centered on Corinne. A few glances wavered in Margot's direction, and all eyes were focussed on her, as their star, with a little wave of her hand in Margot's direction, said very sweetly:

"Some of you have had the pleasure of meeting Miss Anstruther, some of you haven't, but of course you've *all* heard about her fine work as *Conchita,* in *A Toreador's Love!*"

The men bowed to Margot, who gave to each of them a frank, personal smile of acknowledgment, and a slight inclination of her head. Corinne, without another glance at anyone, sat herself on the chair put forward for her, crossed her knees, and beckoned to Margot to sit beside her. It really was amusing, this stardom! If Corinne hadn't acquired the status of star, even her talent—and she had talent—would not have commanded any particular respect from these men, accustomed as they were to rather cavalier methods with the girls in their employ. But Corinne was not only a good little actress; she had her own increasing number of fans, and she was an asset to the Superfilm Company. Margot felt that it. was a definite accomplishment, and she looked at Corinne with new respect.

"Well, Miss Delamar, you wished to have a meeting called to transact some important business. But first let me tell you that Frederick Stoner has run out on us. His resignation reached us this morning."

Joseph Livingstone's small eyes focussed on Corinne. Margot, accustomed to reading human eyes, and finding it easy in so heavy a countenance as that of Livingstone, understood that he was wondering if a love-quarrel between the star and the director were the cause of his sudden resignation.

Corinne turned upon the president a wide, innocent gaze of such complete astonishment—such convincing surprise—that Margot bit her lip, and looked quickly down at her lap. It would be awful if she were to giggle or even smile in the august presence, and at that particular moment. Corinne appeared far too amazed for speech. Joseph Livingstone, apparently afraid of some temperamental outburst, said hurriedly:

"Of course we'll go on just the same. We've got plenty of good directors. And now, Miss Delamar, what can I do for you?"

Corinne's expression changed to frank and disarming friendliness. She said sweetly:

"By doing what I ask, Mr. Livingstone, you will be doing something for your company. I haven't come here to ask a favor for myself. First, I wish to call your attention to the marked talent Miss Anstruther has shown in her work with us. You will agree with me, I'm sure?"

Margot looked at Corinne with an amazement which she had difficulty in disguising. Joseph Livingstone rubbed his beringed hands, and said:

"I certainly agree with you, Miss Delamar. The young lady shows decided promise. We think she has considerable talent."

"Well, Mr. President," Corinne smiled directly at him. "I now want to call your attention to another important point. Miss Anstruther has acquired, in the last few days, much publicity, of a kind that does an actress a lot of good with the public. This publicity will be invaluable, not only to her, but to me and to the whole company. Do you understand, Mr. Livingstone?"

"I get your point." Livingstone's eyes looked suddenly more alive.

"I'm sure you do," Corinne said warmly. "And I'm sure you'll *all* agree with my suggestion that you star Miss Anstruther, just as soon as *A Toreador's Love* is finished!" She threw bright, eager glances around the room.

Margot stared at Corinne in a surprise so intense that she forgot to disguise it, but all eyes were fixed on the star.

"But," gasped Joseph Livingstone, "I was thinking—we all thought—that you and this young lady were not good friends."

"How funny!" Corinne's smile was genius—pure and simple genius, Margot decided. "We're the very *best* of friends, and I admire Miss Anstruther so much that I made up my mind to have a frank talk with you, and try to make *you,* see what *I* see so clearly."

"Well, well, you take me by surprise, Miss Delamar. But, after all, why not? Only we'll have to find a picture for her."

"Oh, that's easy!" Corinne threw her beaming smile once more around the room, then let it rest on Margot. "The title of the picture will be *The Haunting Hand,* and the story will be the mystery of the arm, and the strange lights in her room. It will make a *wonderful* picture!"

"Fine! Fine!" The President again rubbed his white, short-fingered, carefully manicured hands.

There were murmurs of approval, and glances of admiration bestowed on Margot, who sat without a word, far too overcome with genuine gratitude to Corinne for any casual acceptance of her kindness and generosity. A few more remarks, a few more smiles and bows, and the two girls left the board room. Outside they stood still and looked at each other. Margot put out her hand and gripped Corinne's.

"I don't know why you did it, but you're a little brick and I'm honestly so grateful that I haven't words to tell you how I feel about it, Miss Delamar!"

Corinne returned the pressure of Margot's fingers, then she said slowly:

"Well, to be honest, I do like you immensely, and I admire you and your work. You've got real talent. But I suppose—and an honest confession is good for the soul—I suppose that I'm so darn glad you put it all over Stoner, and opened my eyes for fair, regarding his conduct in general, that I felt there wasn't anything too much I could find to do for you. That's the God's truth about it!"

And Margot knew that it was, looking into those strange green eyes with their yellow lights.

In Corinne's dressing-room they found Lulu Leinster smoking a cigarette, stretched at ease in the one comfortable chair. She rose languidly and smiled greetings to the star and to Margot.

Without preamble Corinne went to the point.

"Are you going out to the coast engaged by Stoner?"

The utter amazement in Lulu's large blue eyes was sufficient reply to Corinne's question, without the astonished "No!" that followed.

Corinne flashed a look at Margot, then she said:

"He told me he'd signed you up to go out there. I was sure you wouldn't play me such a trick, but I thought I'd put it right up to you."

"Why, he must be a terrible liar, Miss Delamar, to say such a thing. He *asked* me to go out there and offered me something good if I'd go, but I told him I'd signed up with you and that I'd rather stay here with you."

"Good child!" Corinne patted her hand. "As he's such a picturesque liar, I dare say he lied when he told us he'd seen you and Gene Valery in a night club last night—or rather early this morning." Corinne's inflection seemed to state a fact rather than ask a question.

Lulu's fair skin grew slowly pink and she made a nervous pretense of flicking the ashes from her cigarette. Without raising her eyes she said a little unevenly:

"Mr. Stoner did see me last night with Gene Valery."

Margot's pulse beat suddenly very fast, but her eyes and mouth were under control when Corinne's astonished gaze flew to her, in embarrassed uncertainty.

"Well—" The exclamation came from Corinne in a gasp of annoyance at being put in a false position. "That's funny! Since when have you and Gene Valery been such friends?"

"Why, we're *all good* friends," Margot broke in eagerly, "aren't we, Lulu?"

Lulu gave her a sidelong glance, then she said laconically:

"Sure thing."

"I didn't know," persisted Corinne with a frown, "that you and Gene were *particular* friends."

Lulu said nothing for a second, then she threw Margot an enigmatic little smile.

"Suppose you ask Gene what sort of 'particular' friends we are, Margot. I'm sure he'll tell you. Well—" she turned to the star, "if that's all you want of me, Miss Delamar, guess I'll run along."

Margot gave her an unusually bright smile, but Corinne said rather crossly:

"Run along, by all means."

After Lulu had gone, Corinne threw herself into the easy chair, lighted a cigarette, and asked Margot to sit down.

"Thanks, but I'll have to be running along myself. I can't tell you, Miss Delamar, how I appreciate your interest in me. You're really awfully good to me." The look in her eyes conveyed to Corinne the fact that her loyalty to Margot in the matter of Gene and Lulu had not been wasted.

"See here, my dear." Corinne spoke slowly between puffs on her cigarette. "I wouldn't, if I were you, pay any attention to that 'tripe'—to borrow one of Stoner's pet vulgarities—about Gene and Lulu. If he was with that little mutton-head last night, there was some good reason for it, which he'll tell you quick enough. Don't take it seriously."

"Why should I!" Margot laughed, with a gaiety that did not deceive Corinne. Then she said good-by and departed.

On her way to the train she deliberated whether or not to take any initiative where Gene was concerned. The suspicion had come to her, that he was angry and hurt, far more seriously than she had imagined possible—that is, assuming that he was sincere in his protests of love for her. A faint doubt on this point pricked her consciousness with uneasy reminders of

Lulu's enigmatic smile. Could it be possible that Gene was like the majority of men!

At last Margot faced the unpleasant conviction that she was miserable at the very idea of Gene's insincerity being a possible factor in the situation. She shrank from acknowledging to herself that she felt jealousy of Lulu Leinster, for jealousy is an admission of inferiority. But it actually came to that, if she were to be honest with herself. She *was* jealous—horribly jealous—and miserable as she had never supposed she could be over a man.

Well—she'd been rather silly, playing a waiting game with Gene, and pretending not to take him seriously, and it was up to her to give him the benefit of the doubt. She'd send for him and ask him frankly about Lulu. If, in so doing, she would run a risk of showing Gene how much she really loved him, surely it was worth the risk. She sent him a telegram from Astoria to come and take her out to dinner, then she hurried back to town.

CHAPTER XVII

"BETTER THAN BROTHERLY!"

The door of Margot's room shut out the rest of the world, and she and Gene stood looking at each other.

He had come at her bidding, a little reluctantly it had seemed to her, but she had greeted him with gay insouciance and had delicately skirted the edge of personalities during the dinner hour.

She had told him of the encounter with Stoner the preceding day; of his unexpected appearance that morning, and his frank avowal of guilt; of Corinne's amazing attitude toward herself, and of the final outcome so far as the president and directors were concerned. She had actually made him laugh with her humorous treatment of events and the persons motivating them. She had caught *I* a quick frown at her description of Stoner's friendly parting with her in Corinne's dressing-room, and her heart had beaten a little faster. Why should Gene frown at mention of Stoner unless he were actually in love with her?

It was all told, and as they stood facing each other, behind her closed door, there was nothing between her and Gene except mutual doubt and suspicion.

"Well," she began lightly, sparring for time, "I hope I didn't butt into any of your plans for this evening by sending for you, Gene."

"Is that supposed to be funny?" he said sternly, looking at her with unhappy eyes.

"'Funny!'" She gave a nervous laugh. "Why, no. I'm quite serious. Come on, let's sit down. I hate talking standing up."

She moved to the divan and he took a chair a few feet away and sat down a little stiffly, Margot thought.

She saw that he was not going to help her out, and with sudden irritation she said abruptly:

"I thought *possibly* you might have an engagement for to-night with Lulu Leinster."

He bent forward and looked at her intently.

"So—that big stiff, that cad, told you he saw us last night."

"He mentioned it—casually." Margot tapped the end of an unlighted cigarette with elaborate unconcern. Then she flashed him a sudden glance of assumed surprise. "Why was it such a horrible faux-pas for him to have mentioned it?"

"You know that wasn't what I meant," Gene said quietly. "Some other man might have mentioned a thing like that— 'casually,' as you call it—but not Stoner. He had some mean motive or he wouldn't have bothered to talk about us."

"Well—perhaps," Margot conceded slowly. "However, the interesting fact is that you *were* with Lulu last night. You see, Stoner told us that, Lulu was going out with him, or after him, to the coast, and it seems that Corinne had signed her up for her next picture, so she was sure Stoner had lied. She sent for Lulu and questioned her, and to my annoyance asked her if it were true that Stoner had seen you two together last night. Lulu said it was. So that was that. I'm just amused, you know, for I hadn't supposed you cared enough for the little prize beauty to spend an hour with her, voluntarily."

"You know damn well I don't." Gene's unexpected violence was rather startling. He stared at her with somber eyes.

"Then what, may I ask, just in passing, happened to bring about the little party last night?"

"See here, Margot, I don't know that you have the right to question me, considering your *sisterly* interest in me, but I'll tell you what there is to tell, because I'm fool enough to care tremendously what you think of me, regardless of loving me."

Margot lowered her eyes quickly. She was afraid of what Gene might read in them, and she wasn't quite ready for her own confession.

"When I left you, night before last, I made up my mind that I couldn't stand your little cat-and-mouse game any longer. Something rose up in me against your treatment of me. I couldn't stand it any longer," he repeated himself helplessly. "It seemed to be clear enough that you didn't and never would care for me as I wanted you to. I was pretty miserable. Last evening I happened to run into Lulu on Broadway. It struck me she wasn't looking very cheerful herself. On a sudden impulse I asked her to spend the evening somewhere with me. She agreed. I admit, frankly, I tried desperately hard to work up a flirtation with her. She realized just what an effort I was making and she laughed at me. Finally she got me started about you and I spilled over, told her everything and she gave me the sympathy I needed. That's all there was to it, Margot."

She studied him for a moment, then she said gently:

"Are you sure that's all there was to it, on her side?"

Gene gave a sudden laugh. *"Ask* her," he said briefly. "Why, she's so in love with some nut in the company, who's got a wife and three kids, that she can't *see* any other man. I gave a little good advice and I believe it got under her skin. Hope so, anyway."

With her heart beating faster and her eyes glowing with excitement, Margot tried to speak calmly.

"Do you remember my saying that after disposing of Stoner and my mystery, there was something else of importance I had to attend to?"

"Yes, I remember," he said, frowning at her. "Something of vital importance, before you could pay any attention to *me*."

She smiled at him, mockery on her lips, tender challenge in her deep gray eyes. He got up quickly and stood looking down at her, where she lay against the cushions.

"For God's sake, Margot, stop playing with me!"

"Silly, silly old thing!" she said softly. "It never remotely occurred to you that the 'important' thing I hinted at so mysteriously was—well, my dear, just—you and me."

He threw himself beside her and leaned over her, speaking fiercely.

"You said you'd let me kiss you as a *brother*, and for the last time. What the devil did you mean?"

"I meant—that the next time you kissed me, I'd want it to be as—my lover. Then you became a caveman, and—and I *liked* it, but you banged out of the room without waiting to find out."

He stared at her a second, then he gave a low cry and seized her in his arms. He kissed her, eyes and throat and mouth, in an ecstasy of joy and of passion long restrained.

"Darling—darling! I never dreamed—I was afraid even to hope. I love you so, Margot, I adore you."

Between his kisses she managed to tell him that she had known beyond all possibility of doubt, just how deeply she loved him, when he had given way to his emotions, in that very room two nights before, and had kissed her as no man had ever kissed her before and as, she could assure him, no *other* man would ever kiss her.

"I didn't have to kiss you to know what I felt for you." He studied her face with rapturous intentness. "Women are funny. A man wants to kiss a woman *because* he loves her, or rather *if* he loves her, and a woman loves a man because he kisses her."

Margot laughed. "Not quite that, dear. Stoner didn't arouse my passion by kissing me."

Gene drew her closer with a sudden access of possessive jealousy.

"Damn Stoner. Don't remind me that he ever touched you."

"That reminds me," she said softly. "Another awakening I had in regard to my love for you, Gene, was when I suddenly realized I was miserably jealous of Lulu. Then I *knew,* even better than I did after your caveman exhibition, how much I loved you."

"I'm terribly flattered, darling, but it does strike me as grotesque, being jealous of that girl. However, I'm mighty glad I ran into her the other night, if it made you a little surer of your love for me."

The first hour of love's abandonment to the joy and thrill of mutual understanding, made the blood tingle in Margot's cheeks, and her lips were tremulous and moist with the first tempest of emotion she had ever experienced. At last she drew a little out of her lover's arms and studied his eager, sensitive face. Suddenly a smile drew up the corners of her mouth, and she put soft fingers against his lips.

"I'll believe anything, anything at all you tell me, about adoring me and how beautiful I am, but don't you dare ever tell me again that I could never grow old or ugly in your eyes."

He laughed and pressed his lips against her hair.

"But it's the truth. Perhaps we'll both live long enough for me to prove it to you, sweetheart."

"And there's just one other thing I'd rather not have you say, Gene. Tell me you love me, as often as you like, but never say you'll *always* love me. Men are always telling women that, and how can anyone promise such a thing! Live it, Gene—by all means *live* it—but don't *say* it. It might spoil our luck."

"Fat chance," he said, with more eloquence of tone than of language.

"By the way, Gene." She gave him one of her brilliant roguish smiles. "It'll be rather nice, after we're married—I won't have to call you by phone if I should get scared by a spook."

"You little devil!" He gave her a quick hug. "You whimsical darling!"

"'Whimsical,'" she repeated softly. "That's rather nice. You never called me that before."

"Haven't I? Well, I've often thought it. It describes you better than anything else. It's the thing about you that will never let you grow old or ugly. I *will* say it, for it's true. It's the thing so few women possess, and that charms and holds a man longer than beauty or wit or even," he added with a laugh, "a good disposition, and God knows that's important enough."

"Here, here! I guess, after all, if that's the way you feel about it, I'll let you say—just this once—that you'll love me forever and ever."

And Gene's reply, swift and silent, far better than a brotherly kiss, was more eloquent than any words could have been.

OTTO PENZLER'S
LOCKED ROOM LIBRARY

FROM MYSTERIOUSPRESS.COM
AND OPEN ROAD MEDIA

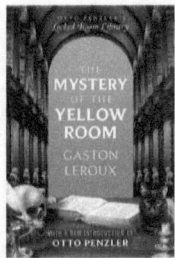

MYSTERIOUSPRESS.COM

Otto Penzler, owner of the Mysterious Bookshop in Manhattan, founded the Mysterious Press in 1975. Penzler quickly became known for his outstanding selection of mystery, crime, and suspense books, both from his imprint and in his store. The imprint was devoted to printing the best books in these genres, using fine paper and top dust-jacket artists, as well as offering many limited, signed editions.

Now the Mysterious Press has gone digital, publishing ebooks through **MysteriousPress.com**.

MysteriousPress.com offers readers essential noir and suspense fiction, hard-boiled crime novels, and the latest thrillers from both debut authors and mystery masters. Discover classics and new voices, all from one legendary source.

FIND OUT MORE AT

WWW.MYSTERIOUSPRESS.COM

FOLLOW US:

@emysteries and Facebook.com/MysteriousPressCom

MysteriousPress.com is one of a select group of publishing partners of Open Road Integrated Media, Inc.

THE MYSTERIOUS BOOKSHOP, founded in 1979, is located in Manhattan's Tribeca neighborhood. It is the oldest and largest mystery-specialty bookstore in America.

The shop stocks the finest selection of new mystery hardcovers, paperbacks, and periodicals. It also features a superb collection of signed modern first editions, rare and collectable works, and Sherlock Holmes titles. The bookshop issues a free monthly newsletter highlighting its book clubs, new releases, events, and recently acquired books.

58 Warren Street
info@mysteriousbookshop.com
(212) 587-1011
Monday through Saturday
11:00 a.m. to 7:00 p.m.

FIND OUT MORE AT:

www.mysteriousbookshop.com

FOLLOW US:

@TheMysterious and Facebook.com/MysteriousBookshop

OPEN ROAD

INTEGRATED MEDIA

Find a full list of our authors and
titles at www.openroadmedia.com

FOLLOW US
@OpenRoadMedia